W9-BNQ-035

ALSO BY YASMINA REZA

PLAYS

Conversations After a Burial
Théâtre Paris-Villette, Théâtre Montparnasse (1987);
Almeida Theatre, London (2000)

The Passage of Winter
Théâtre du Rond-Point, Paris (1990)

Art
Comédie de Champs Elysées (1994); Wyndham's Theatre, London (1996);
Royale Theatre, New York (1999)

The Unexpected Man
Théatre Hébertot, Paris (1996); Royal Shakespeare Company and
Duchess Theatre, London (1998); Promenade Theatre, New York (2000)

Life × 3
Burgtheater, Vienna (2000); Théâtre Antoine, Paris (2000); Royal
National Theatre, London (2000)

OTHER WORKS

A translation of Steven Berkoff's version of Kafka's *Metamorphosis*,
directed by Roman Polanski

Hammerklavier, a novel

Lulu Kreutz's Picnic, a film, directed by Didier Martiny

DESOLATION

DESOLATION

Yasmina Reza

TRANSLATED FROM THE FRENCH BY CAROL BROWN JANEWAY

·

Alfred A. Knopf New York 2002

Thanks to Alex

THIS IS A BORZOI BOOK PUBLISHED BY ALFRED A. KNOPF

Translation copyright © 2002 by Carol Brown Janeway

All rights reserved under International and Pan-American Copyright
Conventions. Published in the United States by Alfred A. Knopf,
a division of Random House, Inc., New York, and simultaneously
in Canada by Random House of Canada Limited, Toronto.
Distributed by Random House, Inc., New York.

www.aaknopf.com

Originally published in France as *Une désolation* by Éditions
Albin Michel S.A., Paris, in 1999. Copyright © 1999 by Éditions
Albin Michel S.A. and Yasmina Reza.

Knopf, Borzoi Books, and the colophon are registered
trademarks of Random House, Inc.

Library of Congress Cataloging-in-Publication Data
Reza, Yasmina.
[Désolation. English]
Desolation / by Yasmina Reza ; translated from the French by Carol
Brown Janeway.—1st. American ed.
p.   cm.
ISBN 0-375-41087-2
I. Janeway, Carol Brown.   II. Title.
PQ2678.E955 D4713 2002   2002016263

Manufactured in the United States of America
FIRST AMERICAN EDITION

DESOLATION

The garden—all me.

The word is, you have a good gardener. People say to me, You have a good gardener! What gardener?! A laborer, a workman. He carries things out. You, you do the thinking. Him, he pushes the wheelbarrow and he carries things out. Everything—I've done everything in the garden. People congratulate Nancy on the flowers. I decide on the color scheme and the plants, I site them, I buy the seeds, I buy the bulbs, and her, what does she do?—it gives her an activity, you'll tell me— she plants them. People congratulate her. That's life. The celebration of the superfluous.

I'd like you to explain the word *happy*.

Desolation

On Sundays I talk about you with your sister, because I talk about you. You, you think I don't talk about you, but I do talk about you. She tells me, He's *happy*.

Happy? The other day, at René Fortuny's, some idiot said, "Surely the purpose of life is to be happy." On the way home in the car I said to Nancy, "Did you ever hear anything so banal?" To which Nancy's subtle response was, "So what should it be, according to you?" For her, happiness is legitimate, you know. She's one of those people who think happiness is legitimate.

Do you know her latest accusation? I had a new roller blind made for the laundry room. You know how much the guy wanted to charge me to install the Japanese shade I could buy readymade in any supermarket? Two hundred twenty dollars. I object. I'm not looking to get robbed, you know. Finally, the guy, who's a robber, knocks off $40. You know what upsets her? That I spent a hour and a half getting him down $40. Her argument? You reckon you're worth $40 an hour. Trying to make me mad. And her other argument? The guy has to earn a living. That's how she is.

So you're happy. At least that's what they say.

People say you're idle, people say you're nonproductive, and then they say, He's *happy*. I've fathered someone happy.

I, who strive to achieve some modest contentment in the middle of this pleasant flowerbed, I spawned a happy man. I, who was accused, principally by your mother, of tyranny, most especially with regard to you, accused of excessive severity, of injustice three times out of five, I stand here today in contemplation of the good—the excellent—results of my educational efforts. Granted, I didn't foresee the hatching of a contemplative being, but isn't a father's desire the happiness of his family?

Happy, your sister says. He's thirty-eight, and he crisscrosses the world on the 99 cents he gets from subletting the apartment I rent for him.

Crisscrosses the world. Let's face it. . . .

I say, "What does he do? In the morning he steps out of the bungalow. He looks at the sea. It's beautiful. Okay, I agree, it's beautiful. He looks at the sea. Fine. It's twelve minutes past seven. He steps back into the bungalow, and eats a papaya. He goes out again. It's still beautiful. Thirteen minutes past eight . . . and then?"

Desolation

What happens then? That's when you have to start telling me what *happy* means.

You're looking well. Good weather in Mombasa. Mombasa or Kuala Lumpur, I don't give a shit, don't let's get bogged down in details. It's all the same to me. After thirteen minutes past eight, East or West, the world is you.

Hats off, my boy, one generation and you've wiped out the only credo by which I've lived. I, whose only terror is the daily monotony, who would swing open the gates of Hell to escape that mortal enemy, I have a son who samples exotic fruits with the savages. Truth has many faces, your sister said to me in an upsurge of idiocy. Indeed. But truth in the guise of a papaya-sucker is opaque, you know.

It would be hopeless trying to find the slightest trace of impatience or restlessness in you, you sleep, I imagine, you sleep like a log, you don't belong to the band of wanderers who pace the predawn streets and are my friends, it would be hopeless trying to find a hint of futile anxieties, inchoate restlessness, in a word — unease. I'm not even sure you understand why I'm concerned about you. That I can worry about your lack of worry must strike you as a new phase of my monomania, no? You wonder why I don't relax, you say to yourself, What does he do with his days, in a state of perpetual metamorphosis, what's the sense of it, never sated, never appeased. Appeased! Don't know the word. My son, any man who has tasted action dreads fulfillment, because there's nothing sadder or more washed out than the accomplished act. If I weren't in a constant state of metamorphosis, I'd have to battle the gloom that comes with endings because I refuse to wind down in some female fit of the vapors. At your age I knew about conquest, but more important, I already knew about loss. For you see I have never had any desire to conquer things in order to keep them. Nor to be some particular person just to stay that way. Quite the opposite. As soon as I settled on a self, I had to undo that self again. Only be whoever you're going to be next, my boy. Your only satisfaction lies in hope. And now my offspring opts to be becalmed in a slack prosperity based on utter lack of ambition and wandering all four points of the compass. Basically, if I've never dared to attack happiness, and I mean attack, please note, as in assault a fortress, you don't conquer a fortress by lying in the sun eating papayas, if I've never attacked happiness, I say, it's maybe because it's the only state you cannot fall out of without hurting yourself. It's a glancing blow but you never heal. You, poor sweetheart, you want peace right away. Peace! When it comes to vocabulary, let me do the honors. To be precise, it's well-being. You want to turn into a piece of seaweed as fast as you can. You're not even trying to fake some spiritual infatuation, I could be taken in by that, I'm not un-naïve. No. You come back tanned, calm, smiling, you sent two or three anodyne postcards and people who want to please me—want to please me!—say, He's *happy*.

When you were a child, you groveled at my feet for months because you wanted a dog. Do you remember? For months you groveled, you cried, you begged, you asked over and over again. I said no, categorically, you kept on nagging. One day you uttered the word *hamster*.

You had swapped the dog for a rat. I said no to the hamster and earned myself the right to hear the word *fish*. You couldn't sink any lower.

Your mother persuaded me to agree to fish, and we had the aquarium.

Were you happy with the aquarium? I pitied you, my boy.

· · ·

You see these primulas, sluts, they're choking the leeks, nobody thinks of doing any weeding. If I don't take care of it, with my back that's killing me, nobody will. You have to be nice to the maids, according to Nancy. Nice means not asking them to do anything. Recently she said, If Mrs. Dacimiento quits, I quit too. Under the pretext that I wasn't being sufficiently nice to Mrs. Dacimiento. Whatever Mrs. Dacimiento's faults or qualities—of which she has fewer and fewer—I am supposed to curb myself because she is a servant. So what if Mrs. Dacimiento is now mediocrity-made-flesh, someone who can neither climb stairs nor bend over, Mrs. Dacimiento can't even raise her eyes or lower them, she can only see the world at her own level. She's married to a man who installs central heating, a stay-at-home who hates everything. Doesn't even like football on TV. Which is weird for a Portuguese. The Portuguese like big balls, fat, and car catalogs. Hers likes nothing.

If I listened to my inner self, I have no idea how I'd be. This woman has been living with us for seven years. In seven years, she has not once figured out how to fit the garbage bag properly over the rim of the garbage can. Sometimes I long to say, "Have you never put a rubber on a guy?" Have you seen how bloated I am these days? I disgust myself. Eat too much for lunch, not enough in the mornings. Always hated breakfast, hated the ritual. That endless show of vitality. Nancy is always in a good mood in the mornings. She smiles as she pours your tea. As she crunches her little piece of buttered toast with honey her eyes are marking out the hidden boundaries of her day. She's wonderful, you know. She loves people, she wants the best for all humanity. Starting at dawn. The woman is so upbeat, it's a nightmare, from the moment she gets out of bed. Granted it's new, but that's how it is from here on out. Nancy's on the side of generosity. At any given moment she's doing her utmost to talk people into submission, and at the first opportunity she hurls herself into the nearest crowd waving slogans and all the rest of it. She wasn't like that when I got to know her, as you can imagine. The idea of democracy gave Nancy the raw material to elevate her soul. Maybe what she lost in sex appeal she made up in paradise? Nancy overflows with energy. She accuses me of constant complaining, she doesn't understand that a man who has no place to whine cannot be a normal man. She accuses me of never helping her, she accuses me, whenever we go somewhere, of collapsing on the bed while she does the unpacking, she doesn't understand that I'm always more tired than she is. Even when she's tired, she lacks any taste for the horizontal, whereas me, I'm from a long line of the spread-eagled, distinguished by our renunciation of our stomach muscles. Nancy knows nothing about the aging of the body, just as she refutes any element of the tragic in life. Which two things are identical, come to that. Since she's started getting passionately involved in social upheavals, and since she's turned her dacimientesque inclinations into a way of life, Nancy is thrilled to be a member of the human race. I am surrounded on all sides by an army of the happy, as you can see! When I got to know her, she was exciting, and at least she didn't fling herself gaily into the thick of existence. You could detect a little trace of melancholy in her manner. A little existential pallor. Very exciting. A lack of will is a tangible quality in a woman. When I got to know her, I can even say that from a certain standpoint Nancy was superior to me. What has dulled itself into indifference in me—worn down by tiredness, old age, and, if I boast a little, by defeats that I myself sought out—she already had by sheer stupidity. The essence of stupidity. That is how desirable women are, my boy: a little superficial, a little absentminded, inclined to nebulous ideas. You cannot imagine how terrifying the change is. A heart that you thought was languishing, a body that you thought was tender and reserved for your own debaucheries, are seized in the brutal grip of optimism and transformed into the heart and body of a squadron leader. A brain that you thought was bound to apathy starts to manufacture thoughts, and of course the thoughts are always contrary to your own, and uttered pigheadedly, just to finish you off.

Explain traveling to me. My child. I understand the longing to move. I understand about restlessness. I understand the curiosity, the desire to be something other, that last in particular. Before I became the old man you see, I found all that with women. I'd be someone else for two or three days. Boring. Are you someone else on your odysseys? Tell me, teach me, what goes on *way* away out there. Way away from what?

·   ·   ·

The garden—all me. If I dropped dead in it right now, in two months it would be a wilderness. Lionel's wife changed the curtains in their apartment. I have Lionel on the phone every morning, and every morning since the catastrophe Lionel tells me about the catastrophe of the curtains. Imagine a man who has spent forty years yanking the same curtains closed and who suddenly in the last stages of his life finds himself forced not only into change but also into gentle arm movements because his wife has decided to spruce up the place and has installed a sliding track for the new curtains he loathes. Take Lionel as an example; Lionel has always been a sort of contemplative creature. Nobody could say, could they, that Lionel had thrown himself into life's great adventure? And equally you could say to me, Why do you forgive Lionel for having spent the best of his days staring out of his window at Place Laugier-Farraday when you blame me for observing all the magic of our planet? To which I would respond, dear boy, that Lionel has never, ever aspired to the least hint of fullness, a ridiculous word by the way, to the least hint of prosperity, to even an atom of bodily satiety. Lionel, who was always nailed to the spot by pessimism and inner torments, has only one aspiration, which is peace of mind. A terrible ambition, my child, and one that has no need of the Antipodes. But I have to tell you that if Lionel has become the friend he is, it's because at any moment when I might be assailed unexpectedly by dark fantasies, I will find in him some echo, even a contradictory one, of my dejection. You cannot be friends with someone who's a happy man or who wants to be, which is even worse. For starters, you see, you don't laugh with a happy man. You *can't* laugh with a happy man. For starters, I don't even know if a happy man laughs at all. Do you laugh? Do you still laugh? Perhaps, contrary to all allegations by your cow of a sister, you're not definitively happy?

With Lionel, I laugh. And I laugh uninhibitedly. And I sympathize with him. And I understand the tragedy of the curtains. And because we understand the tragedy of the curtains, we can also laugh about it. But there's nobody else Lionel could laugh with over the curtain catastrophe. If we can laugh about it, it's because the two of us have weighed the disturbance. A weight, you'll admit, that a happy man has no means to assess. Besides, a happy man is happy to change the curtains because he craves transformations. A happy man consciously chooses a woman who changes the curtains. Where Lionel and I see a criminal, normal people who aspire to happiness salute a balanced woman and a sane one. A domestic Nancy. Mrs. Dacimiento leaves for eight days in Portugal at the beginning of November. The beginning of November: a date she concocted herself. Supposedly her central-heating guy is marrying off his sister. It's nonstop in these big families: if it isn't a marriage, it's a funeral. And Nancy applauds. That Dacimiento decides, a cappella, to take a week's holiday right in the middle of the year and without giving us more than a month's warning or asking our opinion, God forbid she should ask for our authorization, all this strikes her as perfectly legitimate and congenial. Fine. But that I could dare to express a slight reservation about the appropriateness of defining November as a normal month when Dacimiento has already taken her vacation and her paid days off and she'll get her Christmas bonus and the central-heating guy will get most of my pants and my shirts, sooner or later, is a manifestation of mean-mindedness and psychological inadequacy that stuns her. The new charter of her existential positivism has an obligatory clause in it mandating the dropping of your pants in front of the maid.

Your sister, whose choice of words is always calculated to annoy me, says that you *taste* things. To me, tasting things means Denise Chazeau-Combert sucking on a caramelized cherry. She tells me you taste things, which naturally implies "as opposed to you, Papa." Besides, the "as opposed to you, Papa," is part and parcel of 90 percent of whatever the two of you say. What are you tasting, my child? What are these faraway things that are worth a dalliance?

In Place Laugier-Farraday, there's a tree. A chestnut, I think, but I'm not sure. In short, a single tree that Lionel's been looking at from his window for forty years. Every day, in every season. Buds, leaves, fall, and so on. Every day, in every season, Lionel has observed time's shattering indifference.

In a single generation you have swept away the only credo that has ever motivated me. I whose only terror is daily monotony, I who would push open the gates of Hell to escape such a mortal enemy, I have a son who's rotting in leisure. Maybe you knew from the beginning—what a piece of wisdom, if that's the case!—that we're all condemned to be inferior to ourselves. The world shrivels me day by day. And though I have struggled relentlessly but in vain against this desiccation, it was a battle lost before it began. So, you'll say, secure in the wretched mishmash of commonplace mediocrity that seems to be your substance, was there any point in joining battle at all? Because any war, no matter how pointless or how deadly, is better than mere comfort. In the course of my life I have been literally killed, first imprisoned then executed, by the inertia of people whose only goal is comfort. Your pals. The horde of people just like you. What amazes me about you is that you haven't embarked on a little family. Like your sister. The first woman, parenthetically, ever to give birth to a child. And, while we're at it, how are you doing with women, dear boy? You screw a little on your voyages? You do screw, don't you?

Explain to me about voyages, my boy. Is there a life outside oneself? Is there a reality outside oneself? The only woman who ever truly obsessed me was a slut who wasn't fit to tie my shoes. I would have torn myself to pieces for her, and in one sense she skinned me alive. It was my only existential experience. She was simply there, like an object, worthless, persisting in being worthless, but her yeses or her nos could reduce me from a conqueror to a bundle of rags, when she said yes I could challenge the universe and when she said no I crumbled.

Life is our impatient desires. Reality is what has to give way. That's my theory. The rest is women's nonsense.

Tell me about traveling. I used to go off myself, if you remember, when the two of you were children. My annual trip to the *Far East*. For years I said *Far East* when I meant Korea. Then, business expanded to include all Southeast Asia, when I got into manufacturing I went to Hong Kong, Singapore, Macao, in short what's the difference? Hotels, factories, offices, business lunches, airports, hotels, palm trees, American cars, factories, planes, evenings of entertainment laid on by the suppliers, dancing in your stocking feet with some kind of geishas who've fed you beforehand with little sticks like an infant, not whores but not virgins either, city tours, monuments you don't give a shit about, you come back with a suitcase stuffed full of junk, knick-knacks, and all that souvenir rubbish, and what world have you seen, where have you been, those simple words *Far East* contained so many more boundaries, so many dreams, so much more of a voyage!

Her name was Christine, she called herself Marisa. Her advantage over your mother and Nancy is that she never tried the American thing, if you see what I mean. Your mother and Nancy transformed themselves into Americans over time. It was the only way they could find to distinguish themselves. Emancipation. I knew your mother had turned into an American the day I heard her at dinner casually mentioning, excuse the detail, toes and earlobes as erogenous zones. Those last words uttered in the uninhibited tones of a woman who uses them as part of her daily vocabulary.

Unhappy—yes, I was unhappy. In some absurd way haunted, in some absurd way shattered. Shattered by Marisa Botton, alias Christine, in charge of planning and contract administration at Aunay-Foulquier.

She lived in Rouen. All our clients at the beginning were in Rouen. The Montevalons, the Köllers, Aunay-Foulquier, Rouen.

Marisa Botton, Rouen. The only reality, Rouen.

Final quarrel with Arthur. Over a phrase. Talking about René Fortuny, I said, "René has no taste."

Desolation

"He doesn't have your taste," Arthur retorts.

I say, "You've seen that hideous living room of his."

"Say you don't like his place, don't say it's hideous."

"What's the difference?"

"Will you please," pontificates Arthur, "will you please make a distinction between your imagination and reality."

Subtext: you're not the whole world. There are things in their infinite variety, and then there's you, you episodic little piece of shit, and no one gives a fuck about you or your opinions. As a result of which, I quarreled badly, irreparably, with Arthur, whom I won't miss for a minute you might say, except for chess, where although his game had gone off, he proved to be the only possible partner. Way off. You couldn't play a quick match with him anymore. His neurons were all shot to hell. A guy who bases his priorities on so-called reality has lost his intellectual level anyhow. To look at it a different way, a guy who fails to take the hideousness of René Fortuny's living room as a measure of reality is a guy who's had it. And, final remark, will you please make a distinction between reality and your imagination. Completely absurd. Total failure to grasp the universe. What has happened to Rouen since this name stopped breaking my heart? Rouen that drove my every action, my every gesture. Rouen, my exile, my Babylon, Rouen, written endlessly, erased, written again, Rouen, surrendered to Arthur's reality, five letters on a roadmap.

One day when we were skiing at Chandolin, while all of you were on the slopes and I was walking along the paths, I met a family of Italians. Mother on toboggan, father on toboggan, children on toboggans. The mother was howling with joy and panic, the father was yelling, "*Frena! Frena!*" The children were laughing, they were all banging into one another, ricocheting off the sides of the track, tipping over in hysterics, *Frena! . . .*

While we were young, we used to go to Morzine in winter, Lionel was engaged to a girl there whom I also liked. From the window we'd watch the sunset on the mountains. Suddenly the girl burst out, "Why do I have such a pessimistic view of life?"

"Look at the mountains," said Lionel. "Look how beautiful the ridges are, one day you'll think, 'I wasted my best hours.' "

"You're right, but what do I do?"

"Be a bit of an idiot."

In Chandolin, the Italians were idiots. Complete idiots on their toboggans. I saw them from a distance on the slope, on their mad descent, falling off, swearing, and me, motionless, an old man that day—I was still young—an old man made of lead and bitterness. Fifty years after Morzine, I said to Lionel, "Did you and I know how to be real idiots?"

"You did," he said.

Lately he confessed that he'd wept at the Place des Invalides as he watched the president of Mexico go past with his motorcycle escort. Lionel wept, undone by the French welcome and the grandeur of the Republic.

"Having failed to be enough of an idiot," I laughed, "you're a genuine moron."

"Of course." He nodded.

Being an idiot, or a bit of an idiot, my boy, doesn't apply to fans of the tropics. Don't misinterpret me. I'm always afraid, you'll forgive me, that you'll try to take advantage of a vocabulary whose humor and lapidary wit escape you. It's the exact opposite, when you think about it. Being a bit of an idiot, as per Lionel's original advice, is only for complicated souls. Only the tormented, you see, which means unfortunately the exact opposite of who you're trying to be, will grasp the brotherly element of choice here. No one urges an idiot to be a bit of an idiot. Nor do they urge it on anyone who's happy-go-lucky, a related idiot, just between the two of us. Even less do they urge it on a truly happy man. If such a man exists.

Lionel can't get it up anymore. "One less curse to cope with," he announces. I say, "So what else is new? You haven't been getting it up for a long time now."

"No, no," he says, "wrong. I can't get it up with Joëlle anymore. With Joëlle it's dead and buried, but I was still managing it elsewhere. The problem is that now I can't get it up with anyone. From one day to the next, it stopped functioning. I didn't have the strength to take it as a real plus. I went to see someone, a Dr. Sartaoui, who's a specialist in this stuff. There were two of us in the waiting room," says Lionel. "I said to myself, Hey, he's younger than me and he can't get it up either. That cheered me up for a moment."

The guy prescribes pills, to be taken two hours beforehand. "Two hours before what," I say.

"Before what? Before you fuck!"

"And how do you know you're going to fuck two hours from now?

"Because with whores you can schedule it, my friend."

Which has always been the biggest difference between Lionel and me. He has a real taste for it, I've never really spent time with them. So—Lionel goes and tests the pill, which is a fabulous success. Second test, just as fabulous, if short-lived. He goes mad. Decides, although he doesn't "go out" anymore and has had no working sense of what goes on out there socially in the city for some years now, to have a fling. He's already located his quarry in a waitress at the Petit Demours where he eats lunch every day of the week. The girl's been working there for a year, and a pathetic bond between them has progressed all the way from jokes to lingering eye contact. Doped up with Sartaoui's pills, Lionel goes over to the direct offensive, an offensive which opens with, "Do you know that in Australia there are black widow spiders in the towns and the yellow snake too, extremely poisonous," this whispered between the blanquette of veal and coffee. Lionel, you understand, has never been with anyone except whores or self-destructive women whom, as far as one can see, he doesn't view in any sexual way but subjugates with his outpourings against love, children, reproduction, in short, life. The waitress—fifty years his junior, please note—belongs to an intermediary category that's completely unknown to him. Which is why this preamble is such a jawdropper.

The girl laughs. The girl laughs and says, as if to show the remark was brilliant, "We've got dangerous animals here as well." Lionel's feathers are in full courtship display, as he feels automatically this means he can propose a rendezvous. The girl accepts. Lionel goes home and starts doing his calculations. They're meeting at 4:30 at a café midway between the two of them, the girl's due back at Demours at 7:00, that gives them two and a half hours, half an hour in the café for verbal preliminaries, 5:00 hotel . . . hotel? Or his place? Which hotel? Lionel opts for his place, which has all the advantages, despite some redundant scruples in the back of his mind which are quickly discarded, so—5:00 at his place, let's say 5:15 to allow for hitches, that means the pill has to be swallowed at 3:15, which means right now, hop, Lionel swallows the pill. He paces around for an hour, rubs himself with perfume, does two or three stretching exercises recom-

mended in one of Joëlle's magazines, decides to sub-
scribe to *Wild Earth*, the publication where he found
his pickup line in Sartaoui's waiting room, and which
is obviously the key to the whole story.

At 4:15 he goes downstairs. He walks up rue Langier
looking much more cheerful than usual, it's a beautiful day, the kind of day when God and the wind have
decided to ruffle you gently on your good side. He's
happy. For four minutes, Lionel strides along as king of
the world.

4:20 p.m. and he's at the café where he orders a
lemon Schweppes, which he loathes, so as to be sure
his breath is fresh. At 4:35 the girl still isn't there, at
4:45 ditto. At 4:55, she arrives. She finds a dazed old
man who holds out a trembling hand. She orders tea
and immediately announces that she'll have to leave
by six. Sartaoui's pill, in defiance of its apparently
shaky user, is sending out its first hidden signals. Disas-
trous timing. The girl is calm, smiles. Listens. Like a
nurse in a palliative care unit. While she's blowing on
her herbal tea, Lionel clutches his chest, the only part
of him that's in synch at this moment, his last wisp of
horizon.

He's going to play his last card.

"I don't feel well," he says. "Something's the matter, could you take me home?"

"You don't feel well?"

"No," he says, struggling pitiably to his feet, "I feel dizzy."

"Dizzy?"

"Yes, dizzy."

She takes his arm. They leave. The rue Pierre-Demours is crowded, noisy. The weather is gray. She supports him in a friendly fashion. Friendly girl, he says to himself, what a farce!

They arrive at the entrance to his building. "Would you like me to come up with you?" she offers sympathetically.

"I'd like that," Lionel answers in a high-pitched quaver, wondering how on earth, once they get upstairs, he will manage to change gears and become Casanova. The elevator comes down. Stops. Picture one of those open elevators with a grille. Lionel sees feet, a corner of skirt . . . Joëlle! Joëlle, general secretary of a pension savings bank at the Porte de Picpus, Joëlle who's been supporting the family for forty years, never in forty years home before seven in the evening, is home today, in the rue Langier, at 5:15.

Desolation

"Madame Gagnion died," she says.

Slut, thinks Lionel, that slut of a Gagnion who finds a way to croak while I'm having a hard-on. Filthy slut. Gagnion is their upstairs neighbor. An old woman who's got nobody left but them. In a word, Lionel thanks the girl, tells Joëlle he too had some kind of attack in the street. What kind of an attack? Joëlle fusses, already in shock because of Gagnion. Nothing, nothing whatever, darling, a little dizzy spell. Joëlle gives some instructions to the concierge, they go back upstairs, Joëlle insists that Lionel lie down. She helps him undress. "But what's going on," she cries, "you've got a hard-on." And immediately, instead of profiting from the situation, starts yelling and hitting him. The bitch from downstairs is nothing but a whore and she'll gut her, he didn't have any kind of attack, he's pathetic, a parasite, a piece of shit. Whereupon farewell Sartaoui, farewell waitress from the Demours, farewell erection.

A finale like any other, you'll say.

Well, yes. One finale leads to another, my boy. First one finale, then the next. Things extinguish themselves one after another. From the glory of day to

the shadows. Like Lionel heading up the rue Pierre-
Demours.

You know that Nancy has also become a psychologist.
You'll say that's all part of her arsenal. She's become a
psychologist and when you come up as the subject,
which happens, this is her theory. I'm supposed to
have traumatized you—a theory your mother naturally
shares—I'm supposed to have traumatized you when
you were a child by my severity, my demands, my
readiness to strike you, and so on. I'm supposed to have
traumatized you and somehow suffocated you. Suffocated you by the force of my personality which was dis-
proportionate to your sensibility, your fragility, your all
those so-called positive words which are in vogue these
days.

So, traumatized and suffocated, you embarked on
life in the worst possible circumstances. To hear tell,
you were on your way to being a drug addict or a delin-
quent. At this stage in the experiment, Nancy thinks
she can arouse my sympathy, which only goes to show
her poor grasp of psychology, by the way. Accordingly
I'm supposed to take pleasure in the fact that you're

laid back. That you have absolutely no ambition, that you'll end up a social disaster—so what. You're a boy who's raising the bar on misery. Hats off. With Stalin for a father, hats off, my boy.

If I weren't moved by some degree of pity and affection for you, I'd find you repellent. Nancy has no idea how much you disgust me when she talks about how *crushed* you are. Those are her words. I'm supposed to have crushed you.

"How?" I ask.

"You were too strong, you didn't let him blossom."

"Ah, but he's blossoming now?"

"Yes, he's beginning to, it's wonderful."

Nancy can talk about you blossoming for minutes at a time. Your crushing and your blossoming are the two major lines on your medical chart. Not once have you ever inquired after my health. To what should I attribute this silence? Shame? Indifference, ennui? You should know I'm not well. And if you've always known I've been prone to illness, you should take on board that they now dictate the way I spend my time. But you don't give a fuck, you don't think it's worth talking about. Your brother-in-law Michel who was here on Sunday with your sister and the baby—that's when she used the word *happy* about you—is blossoming too, go figure. He's joined the Jewish Ramblers at the Île-de-France. The only way he's found to be a Jew at last. Last weekend they did Montfort-L'Amaury-Coignières. They came in the afternoon, in the morning he'd done Montfort to Coignières. Eleven miles. Over the moon. Through colonies of weekend cottages, forests sliced up by highways, the odd hill, what do I know. He's laid back too. No vestige of existential angst. You'll say he's managed to weed-whack his entire psyche at one go. Explain to me how anyone, let alone in a group, can plow all the way from Montfort via Cergy to Coignières, between manure heaps and beetroot fields, ride back on the B line and remain an optimist. Here's a boy who gets up on Sunday after a grueling walk, hops out of bed at dawn's early light, and says to himself, Hey, great, today I'm going to walk to Coignières with my friends the Jewish Ramblers. To Coignières. Apparently one blossoms where one can. You, you need the Caribbean. Because to crown it all, in my despotism and mistreatment of you, I've made you a high-class whore. If you remain immune to the poetry of Cergy-to-Pontoise, it's undoubtedly my fault and I know better than anyone, kindly note, that's it impossible to raise the bar of unhappiness inside the Beltway.

You've decided to take a year's sabbatical. You'll be surprised to know I was curious enough to look up the word in the dictionary, and the definition makes it completely inapplicable to you because it refers to university professors going off once every seven years to do their own research. But so what, if everyone had to avoid abusing or stretching language, nobody'd ever open their mouth. So you decided to take a sabbatical year, a verbal fig leaf to disguise an entire sabbatical life, if what your friends say is to be believed. In short, you've decided to opt out. Fine. If there's anything that interests me, despite myself, in this plan of yours, it's its absolute vacuity. No irony intended, for once. When you decide to opt out of everything except touring the planet, you free yourself of all scruples and parasitic virtues, and clearly you're miles away from any idea, thank God, of devoting your time to some form of good works, like protecting orphaned children or virgin forests. Radically egotistical, radically consistent. That's not so common these days, particularly as someone as weak-natured as you are could be in danger of being dragged into some sort of philanthropic orgy.

. . .

One day your mother opened the newspaper and said, "Leopold Fench is dead."

It was the worst sentence I've ever heard in my life.

Leo Fench was Lionel's cousin by marriage. He had been one of the frontline troops in the heroic epic of mass manufacture in the clothing industry. I don't know if you knew him. At the end of the fifties Leo made a fortune with the introduction of nylon thread that wouldn't ladder. Only two weeks beforehand we bumped into each other on the rue de Solferino. He was coming from the dentist's. No hint of the shadow of death. Pleasant, the same as always. One fine day a man is walking happily along the rue de Solferino and next day he's dead. Leopold Fench was the most cheerful man I ever knew. When we first got to know each other in the fifties, I read this cheerfulness as a form of instability, it takes time to recognize that cheerfulness is a death song. The son of a grocer from Roanne, he made a fortune in nylon and bought himself an apartment on the rue Las-Cases. Main floor and garden, plus another floor upstairs. He had a year's worth of work done on it, maybe even more. He redid the whole thing. He ran all round Paris to find the tiles, he ordered doors from God knows where, and mantelpieces, he went through the decorators, he designed a chandelier himself and had it made in Italy. After a year and a half he moved in with his family. One afternoon just afterward, he calls me. Come by, he says. He opens the door to me himself. We go into the salon. The room opened onto the garden, and you had to go down a few steps. It must have been January, but the weather was particularly fine that day. I tell him, "My friend, it's a triumph." He shows me every detail, I remember we spent whole minutes on the curtain tiebacks with their special pleating, he shows me the size of the rooms, the perspectives, the genuine boiseries, the fake cornices, he shows me everything right down to the light switches. I say, "It's a real triumph." I say, "There isn't another apartment like it in Paris." He nods. We sit down, he on a stool with tapestry work he'd been praising two minutes before. We look at the garden through the glass door. Light streams into the room. There's an occasional noise from the street but it's almost nothing, a vague sound that seems to emanate from the provinces, a background murmur of peaceable life.

Leo watches a leaf quiver, his finger calls my attention to the perfection of some shrub or another and he says, "Now what?"

And that's what I think about when your mother opens the paper and says Leopold Fench is dead. Cans of tuna fish from Roanne, the stool from the rue Las-Cases, his unbuttoned jacket in the sunshine on the rue de Solferino.

A beautiful day, a man walking happily along a street in Paris at the furthest remove from death. The sky belongs to him, the river belongs to him, the houses, and the faces, belong to him, the old friend he meets where rue de Solferino and rue de l'Université cross belongs to him, as, for the last time, although he doesn't know it, does the little chamber that is his life.

Your mother, sounding only marginally surprised, said, "Leopold Fench is dead." The relative unimportance of the death is measured in the offhand way she says it. Your mother has suggested, if not decreed, that the world could keep on calmly turning without Leo, that Leo Fench lived and died the way dogs live and die, nice companions but not important.

Desolation

"I'm shattered by this," I say.

"Shattered? Why? The two of you weren't that close."

"We were close in a way that's beyond you."

"Everything's beyond me these days."

"Quite."

She began to cry. The moment a woman starts to cry, I want to deck her. I can't stand people who go to pieces. Take some cake, my boy. Take a slice. Orange cake, Mrs. Dacimiento brought it for my breakfast. I turned over the plastic wrapping, orange cake, twenty francs. Mass-made by lesbians from Pont l'Abbé in a former pigsty turned factory. That's what she wants to shove down my throat at breakfast, me who hates breakfast. A piece of cellulose spritzed with artificial essence of fruit.

Leo Fench believed in life. And he opted for frivolity because he believed in life, not in people. From people, Leo expected nothing. It was he one day, when Lionel was particularly depressed and was thinking of going to a doctor, who said, "You should take something to cheer you up a little. Just *a little*. Just enough so that you don't seem to be wandering loose all day in Bagneux cemetery."

Leo didn't believe in anything he'd built up himself. Here was a man who had spent his whole life demonstrating how dynamic and risk-taking he was, and he didn't believe in human enterprise or success or the reassuring effects that came with success.

Leo believed in the reality of the chill of the tomb.

Leo believed in the reality of the yellow corridor of Saint-Antoine hospital where his mother died under the supervision of Professor Ottorno, the reality of the time—months—he spent joking about the tubes, the probes, and so on, the whole unfortunate reality of the pathetic mechanics of life.

A man without any illusions about the passage of time, who had the nerve to be genuinely cheerful.

Leo and Lionel were the same age. They started to beat up on each other the moment they got on the telephone. They yelled. You know how it used to end? Joëlle would unplug the receiver for fear Lionel would have a heart attack. Each of them was convinced he looked younger than the other. Whenever the two of them were together, one of them would say, "Tell the truth, which of us looks younger?" and the other would immediately chime in, "Yes, come on, tell the truth, which of us looks younger?" . . .

Desolation

Have you noticed I've been dyeing my hair? I dye my hair. Formula and stylist courtesy of René Fortuny. A failure, huh? I dye my hair. Why? What do I know?

Do you remember this essay topic? You're taking a walk in the woods and you're struck by how picturesque it all is. Some idiot of a schoolboy once wrote *I was walking quietly along the path when all of a sudden, cunningly hidden behind a tree, the picturesque leapt out and struck me.* Do you remember how we laughed? It was the *cunningly hidden behind a tree* that was the best. Well, that's exactly how it's been for me recently with depression. I'm walking along minding my own business and all of a sudden, cunningly hidden in the scenery, depression leaps out and strikes me. With a force and a weight you can't even imagine. And what do I do to fight it? I dye my hair. When existential depression attacks without warning, your father dyes his hair.

Leo on the other hand never dyed his hair. Leopold Fench, prince of the moment, was above that kind of primping. In one day, Leo Fench broke more hearts than René and me in a lifetime. When your mother says in that incredibly tone-deaf way, when your mother says, "Leopold Fench is dead," I think of our last meeting at the rue de l'Université. Two souls encounter each other at random, two paths cross, there's nothing to distinguish them from the rest of humanity, nothing to distinguish them from those who've already lived or those to come. And this, I tell myself, would be totally irrelevant if Leo had not been something I value a hundred times higher than a happy man—a joyful man.

Open the wall cabinet in Nancy's bathroom and you have a perfect vision of human pathos.

Nancy pretends to be aging bravely. For a moment I even feared that her newfound spirituality was going to be the crutch that would allow her to accept wrinkles and facial hair and set off, stick in hand, to wander over hill and dale. No way. Open her cabinet. Cavernous heart of Nancy's secret war against time. You'll trip over my latest discovery in this fortress of lunacy—*Exfoliating Force C Radiance*. A novelty I'd never have noticed if it weren't for the size of the box and its virulent orange color. You know I've never been good at English. *Force C Radiance*. The words terrify me. *Exfoliating!* Poor Nancy, I think. Poor little Nancy, who longs to please for an hour or two before she dies. Poor animal, wearing down her teeth in a frenzy to gnaw the last of the marrow out of life. "But why, Nancy," I say to her, "why all these products? Are they all really necessary?" Nancy shrugs and immediately turns the conversation to the fact that I've dared to enter her strictly private bathroom, and open her strictly private wall cabinet to involve myself, in contravention of the most elementary rules of respect, in her strictly private things. While she's laying down the laws that govern her intimacy for the 412th time, I look at her face, inundated by all the glop from the forbidden cabinet, a nicely sagging face, a face quivering with longing to put it all right, a face advancing peacefully toward its end.

Experience has taught me to be a diplomat, because once you get into territory like this, you know, they're all pretty much out of their minds. One day your mother was complaining about some newly visible sag line on her cheek. Because she was confiding in me, I said, not intending to be mean, quite the opposite: "It's nothing."

"So you can see it too?!" she cries in horror.

"See what? No, I didn't see a thing."

"Don't try and take it back. So it shows, it really shows!" . . . and she's already wailing and turning against me. Since then I've banished "It's nothing" in favor of "It's not true." Whatever "it" is, I deny it. When a woman starts fussing over some physical defect, deny, deny, deny. Particularly if she says, "Tell me the truth." I don't know how things are with you and women, dear boy, but try to keep them in the plural. Don't narrow things down to the singular for as long as you can avoid it.

At the hairdresser, I ask for the same *treatment* as Monsieur Fortuny's, only not quite so strong. I didn't dare say *color* because it's a unisex hairdresser. Result: you can never tell the difference from the way anything was before, except maybe when it's a question of boasting a head of white hair and what comes out is a lunatic blond halo. To sum up, if your hair is dyed it looks dyed, and if it doesn't look dyed, there's no dye in it. That's the truth. Women don't give a shit if they look all tarted up. Women abandoned any idea of the natural centuries ago. But we men, we don't know how to handle all that. The proof is, while I'm at the hairdresser to be shampooed, I'm thumbing through a magazine and I land on Donald Trump and his new fiancée. Blond girl, twenty-five, fine. But as for him, and I put on my glasses to take a better look, he's pushing sixty, hair like an upside-down conch shell, setting off from the back of his head at an angle of 110 degrees, probably to hide a bald spot and landing in a fringed swag on his forehead. The whole thing a tone poem of russet browns. There's a guy who's earning a good living, I say to myself as I wait to be shampooed, a guy who has his photograph taken day and night and hasn't found a single person in his entourage who'll tell him, "No, Mr. Trump, it's not okay, it's *absolutely* not okay." When the girl arrives with her products, I immediately insist on the weaker form of the treatment. René made an easy transition from hair tonic to hair coloring. All his life, René has gone in for creams and scalp massages, and all my life I've envied the hair of René Fortuny.

It's funny the way people set themselves certain goals. René, who from the age of twenty more or less let his body go to rack and ruin, for some reason known only to himself gave all his attention to his hair. Maybe, and I mean this quite seriously, haircare was René's road to the meaning of life.

The world is not outside us. Alas. If the world were outside us, there wouldn't be enough roads for me to travel until I dropped, and instead of hectoring you, I would envy you. I would hate your youth and all the time you have left, and I would envy your eyes, which will see things I shall not see. But the world is not outside us. The world lives within us. Everything you see here, that I planted, my boy, rosebushes, impatiens, boxwood, pear trees, lives only through my thoughts, man's only knowledge of the world comes from within himself and he can never step outside his own skin. Which is why, at bottom, we no longer fear solitude. Even when we grow old and find ourselves alone again, we don't give a shit. Little by little we find ourselves completely alone again and we don't give a shit.

In the mornings, when I'm sitting at table faced with Dacimiento's pound cake and condemned to listen to Nancy crunching her little bits of buttered toast, having already gorged herself on France Inter and *Le Figaro*—fueled by her incomprehensible appetite to be part of the world, she's been ready to cross swords since dawn—I have an actual physical sensation of the solitariness of man's existence. And when your sister thinks to give me pleasure (how am I supposed to forgive her for such utter ignorance of who I am) by telling me "He's *happy*," I calculate how rare the bridges are from one solitude to another.

Desolation

Every day the world shrivels me a little and today it's the world that's shriveling inside me. That's the way things are. Little by little death gains the upper hand. One gets used to it. One gets used to death. It's not such a bad thing to maintain the rhythms of the universe.

In the Kabbalah, which never interested you, doubtless my fault, it says that *one has to shake God to make him show Himself.* Shake God.

You, my boy, you don't shake much, do you?

Shake God.

God *doesn't exist*, but we make space for Him, we take a little step back so that He will come down to our world, not just every day but several times a day and for our whole lifetime. The only reality is His will, for the world, the world, my boy, is made up of our impatient desires.

And what is it you want? What does my son want?

My son wants neither to build, nor to create, nor to invent. Above all, my son doesn't want to change the order of things. My son wants everything to be cool.

At a moment when anything is possible, at a moment when I would have risked my skin to keep my place among the living, my son wants calm and creature comforts, my son wants peace to bandage up the pitiful wounds in his soul. I whose only terror has always been daily monotony, I who pushed open the gates of Hell to escape this mortal enemy, I have given life to a windsurfer.

If you were to tell me to pursue a woman to the ends of the earth, I'd bow. Everything to do with desire is desperate and boundless. The need to be someone else, someone whose dream of being swept to his fate would at last be fulfilled, this I understand. And without setting myself up as an authority on disintegration, I understand one could literally be swallowed up in pursuit of it. In your whole life, my boy, has there ever been a Marisa Botton? If so, you couldn't be happy and nobody would talk about you in such degrading terms, because even if one recovers from a Marisa or someone like her with time, one doesn't come back from it as the same person one was, one is inconsolable, my child, for that part of oneself one has lost, inconsolable.

Marisa Botton from Rouen, in that way, was my true existential experience.

Desolation

To begin with, she was nothing. Absolutely nothing. And she would have gone on being nothing if I hadn't had the idea one day when I was bored, to invent her.

Her name was Christine, and she called herself Marisa. This *Marisa* gave you the whole woman. She was married, with a child. Married to a buyer from Aunay's with whom I did business. That's how I got to know her. At the beginning, completely insignificant. The kind of woman whose dress fits so tightly that she's still pulling on the material to make the skirt or the sleeve sit better. I passed her from time to time in the corridors at Aunay's. One day she says, "It's really irritating," and I say, "Irritating? Are you talking to me?"

"Yes. You never say hello to me. You could at least say hello."

"Do we know each other?"

"My husband is Roland Botton. We had dinner together last winter."

I said hello to her for a year. Because I hadn't recognized her again, I forced myself to recognize her. See what things depend on. Hello for a year. Nothing more. Translate that into twenty hellos if you reckon that I went to Rouen once or twice a month, because due to a phenomenon I put down as sheer chance, I ran into her each time I was there. Twenty hellos, which evolved from hello madame to hello dear Madame Botton and finally, after passing through several variations, ending with Marisa hello! Never an extra word, never a how are you, nothing. The day I said Marisa hello! she stops: "Such familiarity all of a sudden." Why did I throw out Marisa hello!? You know me, nice day, unexpected memory of her first name, probably heard it mentioned five minutes before, in short, a momentary whim and suddenly this woman who didn't exist a second ago, becomes a bodily reality because she decides to take these chance words seriously. "Is that a reproach?"

"Quite the opposite."

She looks me straight in the eye. Incredible cheek. Smiles and goes off somewhere or other. From that day on, I think about Marisa Botton. That's it. But it's enough. It takes a mere nothing, you see, for someone to start making his bed in paradise. Don't clear the table, leave the crumbs, Dacimiento will sweep up. You can't not make crumbs eating this cake. You like the cake, that's good. At least I don't ruin your appetite anymore. You see how I've swelled up? I'm going to croak from intestinal cancer, nobody gives a shit. And

Desolation

I've also probably got Kreutzfeld-Jakob disease, since this morning there's this tremor in my hand. Did you see the stuff she makes me eat? Last night she cooked white beans and ox tongue. Didn't say a word. Ignoring unbelievably filthy looks from Nancy, I told her I was surprised that she'd take a week's paid holiday smack in the middle of the year without giving us more than a bare month's notice. And she starts defending herself, she's been here for seven years, seven years of pure slavery of course, for seven years and she's never once asked for however much it is a month she's supposed to get, she wasn't hired to do the shopping and since she's been doing the shopping her lower back is all shot to hell, she's not even adding in the number of hours she's had to spend because we sat down late to dinner and the central-heating repairman was waiting outside in the car and of course that meant they had to eat dinner even later but they're human beings too, just like we are, and so on. Because they've got nothing better to do but drive to Auchon now and then and sit glued to the TV, cracking peppercorns in their teeth, and suddenly they're talking unions, you know. I'm tempted to tell her they're not even humans, they don't even qualify for the lowest rung on the pretty

damn low ladder of human evolution, and if I manage
to restrain myself it's only due to Nancy's vindictive-
ness because for some time, it's good you should know
this, she's been beating me. Up till now she's always
beaten me in private and I have to say these moments
always make me feel tender toward her again, as if this
temporary madness is taking me back to the fragile
person she was and this unstoppable uncontrollable
meltdown is making me desire her again, but I'm
afraid one day she'll lose it and start to hit me in front
of Dacimiento, all the more because she's been devel-
oping some kind of weird complicity with Dacimiento
recently and isn't far from turning her into her everyday bosom buddy. (What's more, Nancy sent her to
her own hairdresser, I didn't dare say a thing but when
she came back she looked like Richard Widmark off to
the Korean War.) Beating me up in front of Rosa
Dacimiento, a scene I can't rule out, would by the way
have the advantage of giving me the chance to rally
myself and I could throw her out right then and there.
Do they suffer as much as we do? Dacimiento and her
central-heating repairman? Without an imagination,
you can't suffer. What kind of suffering can someone
experience if they only see the world at their own

height, if they can't look up or look down, if top shelves of bookcases and cornices and curtain rods and tops of wardrobes might as well be in the next world, because they're not part of this one? Just as much as *we* do, is what I said. You've taken that in. I refuse to see you as suffering's exile. Even if children don't remain as warm as you think they will, they're still your children and I refuse to lose you completely.

Your sister wants to cultivate me. Odd the way women these days create missions for themselves. She maintains the only thing that interests me is music. True. What's more, to be frank, I can't see the point of the rest. When music takes possession of you, when music fills your life, will you please tell me what's the point of words, even nice ones, what's the point of stories, what's the use of all that imitating life on paper that people are so wild about, and that shows the effort that went into it and the dexterity, and gives you so little sense of inevitability. Your sister told me I'd be less dense if I read. Word for word. I didn't get angry. I'm not upset about being dense. Read what, my sweet? Get to know a little literature, you don't know a thing, you've got the time for it now. Instead of saying the exact opposite, which would have been the only possible way to get me interested in the subject, but her ignorance of who I am is bottomless, you have the time now, she says, instead of saying now, Papa, now that you've no time anymore.

Most of the people I meet, including my daughter, have only the most trivial grasp of time.

Nancy has developed literary pretensions too. More precisely, since I do have to admit she's a woman I've always seen with a book in her hand, pretty much, Nancy has suddenly been captivated by a writer: André Petit-Pautre (you can easily guess what temptations this name sets off in me). You don't know him. Nobody knows him. Except for me, because she sometimes invites him to dinner with his wife. Petit-Pautre is her mentor. And our guest, from now on. I remarked that in a world where everyone writes, it's no surprise that André Petit-Pautre writes too. The other day Lionel quoted me that wonderful thing Enesco said about Bach: *the soul of my soul.* I said to Lionel, who's always loved both books and music, "Can you name a simple text that has been the soul of your soul?"

"No. Words can't reach that high. And the soul doesn't read."

Desolation

I went back to Chopin. I could almost say I took
him up for the first time, because I had hated him so
much for so many years. Aside from a few moments of
Romantic absentmindedness in my youth, I've always
loathed Chopin. And I went back to him thanks to
Samson François, a guy I've never been able to listen
to either before now, because of his name. Samson,
okay, but François! Samson Apfelbaum, absolutely,
but not Samson François. Stuck in traffic, I turn on
classical radio: "Nocturne." I leave it on. It's beautiful.
Here you are, sinking back down to Chopin in your
old age, bravo, I say to myself. Who's the pianist? Samson François. Yet another surrender. What do you
want, I don't care that much anymore.

Your sister who is intent on my achieving cultiva-
tion asked me if I'd been to the Picasso museum. I told
her that not only had I never gone to the Picasso
museum but I never would go to the Picasso museum.
There's too much enthusiasm about him, I said. I hate
the enthusiasm of the masses for *beauty*. Generally
speaking, all these people who haunt exhibitions and
plod around for hours on end revolt me. Your sister,
who's never had a trace of humor or detachment
and hasn't acquired them from her husband either,

though I forgive him because he's a pharmacist and at least I can discuss medicines with him, shrugs her shoulders and asks me with secret sorrow how I spend my days. I think, I tell her, about the absurdity of human effort. You educate people and when you're finally coming down the home stretch what you have to listen to is them proselytizing for literature and the Picasso museum. That's how I spend my days, I tell her emphatically, in these sorts of meditations. "You're interested in politics," says Nancy. "He's always very interested in politics," says poor Nancy, making nice, because my being described as *dense* has upset her and she's not trying to come to my assistance but she does want to rehabilitate herself as a wife. "You're mistaken, dear," I'm obliged to correct her. "I'm interested in events around the planet the way Lionel watches cars and people passing from his window. Which is to say indifferent to everything except the movement." Lumping them together, what never changes about these women is that they never believe me. They take everything I say as a series of pathetic and inappropriate poses. Which encourages me to the worst extremes. I think that by the end of the day, I've asserted, talking about Jerome — oh, yes, Jerome, there's another example, yes, he's my grandson but after all he's only two and a half and sometimes I call him Jeremy or Thomas, which doesn't mean a thing, I hear perfectly well but I just don't hang on to Jerome as his name, your sister takes this as an unforgivable provocation, she doesn't imagine for a second that I could have forgotten the child's name—so, talking about Jerome, I've said what I think, following on from what had become an extended conversation, which is that I'd prefer him to become a tyrant rather than some card-carrying union faggot. Sounds of horrified clucking, and then to close off any recurrence of Dacimiento as a subject of discussion, I state that the only worthwhile system is feudalism, which had the merit of producing either midgets who kept their mouths shut—and didn't go around driving us nuts with the Picasso museum and other cultural flab—or knights and revolutionaries, epic types who wielded the sword and the lance. These days we get placards and balloons and women like you who sing. Me personally, I said again, I prefer people screaming and out for blood, waving pikes. At least they make an impression. "Does getting old involve becoming a caricature of yourself?" your sister interjects to show off her cunning and demonstrate that she's my equal by insulting me. A few years ago I would have slapped her for less. What do you know about aging, you poor creature, how do you even dare use the word after having the complacency to add to humanity by producing a supplementary Jerome. "Getting old," I said with some restraint, "means to be done with compassion."

I finished Sunday overcome by loneliness and despair. I've always imagined despair to be linked to a particular view of life. Today I discover a despair that is independent of time.

Explain to me the word *happiness*. I'm willing to believe there's a part of one's being that provides for it.

I've caught a glimpse of it.

Death is in us. It gradually gains ground. Little by little, everything dissolves and becomes the same. My child, after a certain age, everything is the same as everything else and there's nothing that serves as a goal anymore. And if God, for which I thank Him, hadn't given me such a horror of boredom, I could end up like those old dullards you see sitting on public benches contemplating the victory of time.

Desolation

At the garden show at Longchamp I hear someone say my name. Some unknown woman is smiling at me. Genevieve, she says. Genevieve Abramowitz. She looks like a little tortoise in her summer dress, short hair, eyes still pretty behind her glasses. Genevieve Abramowitz who was once the grand passion of Leo Fench. "I wouldn't have expected to meet you here," she says, "after all these years."

We look at each other for a moment, unable to find the right words. "I didn't know you were interested in gardening."

"I've always had a thing for flowers. I have a house now."

I look at this little lady with her helmet of white hair pulling a little plant wagon full of gardenias and I think of Leo under the earth in Montparnasse cemetery. "And you?" I say.

"I have a pretense at a balcony that I keep spruced up. It gives me something to do."

She says it gives me something to do and smiles apologetically. Immediately I think, me too, it gives me something to do, what else is going on here but me *giving myself something to do*, the two of us are giving ourselves something to do, citizens henceforth of a world in which desire no longer exists. A world in which compost and gardenias have replaced our possibilities of becoming something more. Compost, gardenias, guaranteed exchange rates, little deals here and there, playing the stock market, and getting sick become a substitute for living. A world without a Promised Land, without burns, without victories and defeats, a world where impatience has become terminally beside the point.

O God, grant me the power to relive one day, one hour of the era of obsessions!

Make me a lunatic, a fanatic, a criminal if you want. Give me back a horror of peace and quiet in any form. In the deadly light of the sun at Longchamp stands a man who disgusts me, a worm-eaten creature, a shadow, a man from the suburbs of manhood.

"Every year," she goes on, "I go and leave a stone on Leopold's grave along with a little bunch of violets. His wife wrote me a letter after he died. She knew."

I nod. What is there to say to that? The body can do what it likes, the soul will tell itself any story it chooses. We are only kissing the masks that hide the face of abandonment. The ending of Leo Fench and Genevieve Abramowitz, whom we watched feverish and sleepless: three withered flower stalks and a pebble on a slab.

She knew, she said. I nod with appropriate gravity. Two words which are supposed to re-conjure the illusion, two words to restore some apparent significance to the affair. What did she know, poor thing? What do any of us know, I thought, standing there among the flowers in these hopelessly unsuitable surroundings, since everything effaces itself with the passage of time.

Genevieve Abramowitz gives me news of Arthur, whom, with his wife, she sees regularly. "And you," she asks, "do you still see him?"

"Less than I used to," I say.

"He's just bought an apartment in Israel."

"Arthur? Where?"

"Jerusalem."

"What on earth for?" I yell.

"To spend part of the year there," she answers, astonished.

"I'm appalled."

I immediately think of your brother-in-law Michel, and his discovery of the Jewish Ramblers of Île-de-France, which gives him a system for declaring he's a little bit Jewish. Between genocide and his Sunday exertions he's found a way to weave together his roots and his observances. Michel Cukiermann, my son-in-law: heir of suffering, pillar of the community, contemporary stand-in for the sons of Abraham, disciple of Moses. Which he's turned to account by becoming pro-Palestinian and talking incessantly about peace. Someone you should get on with really well. Listen, I told him, let's settle this once and for all. You want peace in Israel. Okay. Why, one wonders. You want peace over there so as not to mess up relations between Montreuil and Roissy. Ireland, where things have been going on for centuries, doesn't enter your mind, Yugoslavia bores you, you've had it with Kosovo up to here, Rwanda and Cambodia zilch, but you want peace in Israel the same way Arthur has just invested in real estate in Jerusalem. A flag planted for humanism and a little patch of ground for progressive souls in the new territories. That's your way of rebuilding the temple of Solomon.

Genevieve Abramowitz was a very fine woman. A woman with whom you could laugh, which is rare. "I'm appalled," I said to her, "all these Jews without duties, without religious imperatives, buying their own redemption," I go on, suddenly fired up.

She laughs. "You haven't changed."

"Nor you. I always liked your laugh and you still have it. To tell you the truth, I had a row with Arthur. Arthur recently told me to make a distinction between reality and my imagination. Arthur thinks the world can be considered from an objective point of view and that he's the man to do it. The only cause of my unease, according to him, is my incurably partial view of things. He's right. And I'm sure it was a totally objective decision, springing from his absolutely unarbitrary take on reality, when our friend Arthur Sadi, of whom no one could say that he'd breathed the air of synagogues to excess, bought himself a passport to his Jewish identity in the Holy Land."

"But his son just married an Israeli girl!"

"So? If my son marries a girl from Tahiti, which is far from impossible in the circumstances, I'm going to go bury myself in Tahiti?"

"You know that's got nothing to do with it."

"It's worse. He's taking advantage of a marriage which is a surprise in itself, excuse me, Genevieve, to assuage some concocted nationalism that's even more repellent than its genuine twin. Arthur will have a grandson called Ariel or Boaz, which is, I have to admit, certainly better than Jerome, and he'll get into fights with everyone who fails to make the journey to be there for the circumcision. It all makes me sick. Tahiti doesn't lead you that far astray. Tahiti is not an *act*. You have to tell me about this marriage, Genevieve. Because here's a boy I saw being born, whose development I've followed with interest, with whom I always wished that my own son would have made friends, but he refused—you were horribly standoffish, my dear— a boy, all in all, who was infinitely superior to his father and whom, as you can see, I would never have suspected of needing to have his own Jewish girl, let alone an Israeli."

"What's the point, my friend," she replies smack in the middle of the flowerbeds in the park at Longchamp. "What's the point of using all these definitions with me? I'm an old lady now, I'm no longer susceptible to the charms of contrarians like you. You think you're being provocative and you're just being predictable" (your sister used the word *dense*, remember?). "Unlike Arthur I don't think there's any reason to reproach you for the blinkered way you see the world, but why do you feel obliged to belittle it at every given moment? Your standpoint on this story is the standpoint of someone who's fallen out of love. As a standpoint it's devoid of affection, it doesn't carry much authority, if you want to know what I think, and it certainly doesn't merit being broadcast. People we no longer love no longer carry any credit with us and everything they do seems artificial. When we're in love, obviously," she went on after a hesitation, "we blindly cultivate every magic pull of enchantment . . . while you were drawn to Arthur, you would have accepted the apartment in Jerusalem and you would have been happy about the marriage because, please forgive me," she adds by way of a final thrust, "you shouldn't make yourself out to be less of a Jew than you are. You're striking a bit of an attitude."

"My dear Genevieve, last night I was killing time in front of the TV by watching some variety show that was raising money for charity. At a certain moment a singer delivered himself of the pronouncement that 'As long as people love one another, the world will be saved.' I hear this, Genevieve, the words *love* and *hope* being thrown out into empty air and all I want is to declare war on the planet. From a biological perspective, my dear Genevieve, I cannot tolerate any speeches about virtue—I don't mean yours, which is charming and comes from someone who is authentically good and fine (and besides it's not a speech about virtue, it's a reproach)—I told you this anecdote to show you just how incapable I am, alas, of moderation. At the very least I know I should moderate my words. Either keeping quiet or cooling down whatever is boiling inside us should be within the grasp of any civilized human being, but I've ceased to want to play that role, you know, which means I've also ceased doing damage to my health, because always trying to be elegant and balanced was proving fatal for my nerves. No less fatal, to be honest, than the unbridled expansiveness of my moods. So, you see, I'm delivered twice over. Delivered from the paradise of temperance and delivered from the obligation of being in harmony with one's body. No, Genevieve, I would not at some other time have accepted the apartment in Jerusalem. At some other time there would not have been an apartment in Jerusalem, at some other time Arthur would never have given in to the farce of reinventing himself as an exile. At the time you're referring to, Arthur couldn't endure the heat, he hated old stones and bigots, and had no thought of contributing his quota to Jewish history. At that particular time, Arthur wasn't yet considering the world from an objective standpoint, a crowning piece of nonsense, born of who knows what, which is just tolerance by another name. Because that's the word, the defining word at the heart of his speech, *tolerance*. Like a number of people who resemble him, over time Arthur concocted himself a persona of the modern man with his panoply of noble attitudes, his frenzied openmindedness, and his pact with mediocrity. No one is more contemporary than our friend Arthur. That said, Genevieve, you're not wrong to insist that the same act doesn't have the same value when performed by different people. If you yourself were to buy an apartment in Jerusalem, it wouldn't be of any importance to me, any more than a pied-à-terre in Cagnes-sur-Mer, who knows why that came to my mind, I've never said Cagnes-sur-Mer in my life before. In Arthur's case, alas, the proceeding is not a trivial one. Arthur buys in Jerusalem to become a member of a club. The twentieth century has invented the Jew without constraints, without obligations, and without a purpose in life. Here's someone who has lived unwittingly as the hero of his own existence and suddenly, without much of an investment, in his old age wants to become a citizen of all humanity. Member of the club of liberated Jews. What could be more select than that? Zionism and tolerance. Residency and free will. What could be more irreproachable? As for me, who have no desire to belong to any community, I don't want to have a measured step and I don't want to have a measured spirit, my dear, that's the wrong pair of clippers you put in your wagon, let me show you something better and then we'll talk about your balcony."

In the refreshment bar where we find a seat, Genevieve doesn't talk to me about her balcony, she talks about Leo Fench. "One day I got this note from Leo, and I'll tell you right away it's a quote from Louis Aragon which he'd picked up from who knows where because you know, Leo really didn't read much at all (he said he'd read the *essentials* long ago); on this piece of typing paper, folded in four, he'd written, *Don't read this letter: read the other one, the one I tore up. Think about the fact that I'm constantly tearing up a letter, a sort of letter. . . .* Followed by the name of the poet and nothing else. This other letter, my dear, gave me my reason to live for years. And even at this age, taking my grandson to his judo classes or pruning my roses with the wrong pair of clippers, I find myself wanting to decipher words that were never written, never given expression, and never heard. Leo didn't want any part of a romantic entanglement. Love didn't feature anywhere in Leo's rules of life, if I can put it that way. It took me a very, very long time to believe that he could have any genuine feeling for me. You know, one never trusts the words of a seducer. The seducer cannot summon what might be called the moral element in language. In the same way one doesn't dare give way to desire, because yes it's idiotic but one is afraid of not being satisfied sexually (please excuse," she adds, "this excessively confidential conversation which has overtaken me all of a sudden, it's so rare to meet someone with whom I can talk about Leopold and all these things). There are women who boast that they know to keep a man that way. For me, on the other hand, it always made me very vulnerable. In the arms of a man with the reputation of knowing women, one thinks one will be a disappointment or uninteresting. I never imagined I had the slightest sway of that kind over him. Even in our most audacious moments I didn't think I measured up to a Leo Fench, and perhaps this insecurity heightened the excitement. Leo died of a stroke at the age of fifty-seven. A man who had no intention of checking out so soon, who believed even more idiotically than most men in his own longevity. I don't want to brush against you, I told him, I don't want to be a walker through time who brushes against you as our paths cross. But Leopold embraced you even as he vanished into the mosaic of his life. Business, appointments, obligations on the rue Las-Cases, comings and goings of children, his inevitable other women (Leo operated on the principle that a man should seize upon all available women and that all women were more or less available, Leo liked quick sex, no sentiment, no tomorrows) whom I could never think about without feeling faint, trips, vacations, the endless absences that would wound your heart forever. Leo believed, and I still bear him a grudge for this, that we were *imperishable*."

Does it ever happen, my child, in your life of bliss, that you feel the stab of incurable loneliness? In the midst of the gardens in the park at Longchamp, under the deadly spring sun, a woman with whom you have everything in common says something and the words seem to trace a crack and you know there will be no coming together, that it's hopeless, that the soul is solitary and there is nothing one person can do for the other.

She says, "Make me stop. Tell me about your trees, tell me about you, and your life, what are your children doing?"

"My daughter married a pharmacist and I'm a grandfather."

Incongruous phrase which slips out for no reason, but for a moment, in the company of this disarming woman, I give way to spontaneous sentimental vaporings and even produce the name Jerome without having to search my memory.

"And your son?"

"My son loves life and the world," I say.

"What luck!" she laughs. A Genevieve Abramowitz was what I needed. "And you?"

"Me, I've destroyed the best part of myself. I've become more human, and it's tragic, Genevieve." Upon which, I invite her to dinner that night.

We meet up at eight o'clock in the Ballon des Ternes. She's wearing a green suit that matches her eyes, she's discreet, she's pretty, and I'm all dressed up as well. The table I reserved isn't ready, so we have a drink at the bar. I order a whisky, an unusual order for me as you know since I only drink wine, Genevieve orders a gin and tonic. We're both of us, for whatever reason, tongue-tied. I compliment her on the way she looks. She says I've remained a very attractive man. I say I didn't know I ever had been. She tells me to stop flirting. I've honestly never thought of myself as well endowed by nature in that way, and certainly not these days when I'm going to pieces in all directions, but finally all it takes is the littlest thing and you're in the sack. She wets her lips with the gin, I shake my glass to make the ice cubes clink. We smile at each other. The content of this evening is not yet clear. A waiter sets a saucer of shelled pistachios on the counter. "Do you still see Lionel?" she asks. Shelled pistachios, wonderful, I think to myself. "Still. And you?" I take a handful and pop them in my mouth. I'll never know what Genevieve's answer was because my teeth, all set to encounter something with the gentle bite of almonds, have just met an unexpected resistance that is completely and instantaneously disorientating. Simultaneously a glance at the saucer confirms the ghastly truth. I'm in the process of crunching spat-out olive pits.

It's not true, I think, it can't be true. I make a face and spit everything back into the saucer, I take a gulp of whisky—there was foresight in that order—and gargle it noisily, then another gulp, and another, seized with the uncontrollable need to disinfect myself. Genevieve, who hasn't been following all this, stares at me dumbstruck. Between two doses of mouthwash and grimaces of disgust, I point to the saucer and the pits. "My poor friend," she cries, helpless with laughter. "That's horrible." As I glance out of the corner of my eye at the scary clientele of this place, fat sauerkraut-eaters and beer guzzlers, provincial wrecks with grease-smeared mouths, i.e., the assembled pit-spitters, it's her laugh once again that delivers both me and our dinner from everyday wretchedness and its ordinary slot in time.

"I would never have thought," she says once we've been seated at our table, "I would never have thought you'd be the kind of man who'd shut himself off in a house. Let alone the kind of man who'd take up gardening."

"Nancy, my second wife, inherited a house in the Marne from her father. We used to go there from time to time. There are a lot of woods in the area. I like woods. On my side of the family we never had a particular place, I didn't know what it was to become attached to a landscape by habit, walking through familiar trees, walking the same ground, the only variation being a little more to the right or to the left, or taking the longer way round or the shorter. I liked going back there. One day I bought a weeping willow at a tree nursery, then some privet that I planted in the garden every which way. I didn't want to learn, I wanted to create. I dug little holes when what was needed was a hole ten times the size of the root ball, I went mad for manure, things to amend the soil, peat, I spread three bags of manure where one was required, telling myself it was better, I bungled around, I burned everything, but life had substance."

"And rue Ampère?"

"I'm still there. A few days a week."

I tell her I'm still there a few days a week and for the second time that day I feel the black wing of desolation unfurl and settle over me. Is it alcohol that makes the phrase so painful? A few days a week, and for how long? Am I shut off from the future forever? How did it happen? I hate the days. Where are the days, the real days? Stagnation is killing me.

"This is my life. A few days in rue Ampère, a few

days in the Marne, rue Ampère, Marne, the stock exchange, the garden. The ancients used to go off on wars of conquest to ward off tedium. Conquest versus tedium, the bloodied saber versus unendurable peace. Me, I take the train to Châlons and plunge into GardenEarth to buy a manure pitchfork or my umpteenth sprayer. Genevieve, my friend, Genevieve, let's use this evening to fight the grayness of existence. This morning I was thumbing through a magazine article about the correspondence of a Nobel Prize–winning Japanese writer and Oz, the Israeli writer (my daughter wants to cultivate me, Amos Oz has a good place on the lists, she thinks she can lure me with secular-progressive Jewish literature; two pages and I was sound asleep). The title of the article: 'The Battle for Tolerance.' Tagline: the sentence from the Japanese guy, *I hear the note of hope that echoes in your words.* Hope of what, Genevieve? What is it these people hope? The great minds of the century. So absolutely convinced they're on the road to somewhere. So thrilled, poor guys, to be predicting some ultimate achievement (the very idea is grotesque). What is it they hope? What sort of progress? Peace? A horizon with no hidden chasms, no contradictions. No people.

The peace of dead souls. Every day the world shrivels me. A world of word-twisters. Of optimists done up in tutus. Genevieve, I'm crazy about your laugh. Genevieve, what could we scheme up tonight, the two of us? I'm going to order another bottle. Let's drink. Time marches on, nothing is real except this moment. Let's drink and let's laugh. And scheme up some piece of madness. I'm your man tonight."

"Yes," she says sadly, "nothing is real except this moment. Why do the people we love not understand this? I remember there was this song by Léo Ferré, *the beautiful years race by, use them my poor love.* . . . It's impossible to put words to your feelings because every phrase already belongs to another time and everything you find to say is empty and out of date and a lie. My friend, I'll be glad to drink with you this evening as much as you want, but since you love my laugh, look at this for a catastrophe, my eyes are full of tears."

I long to stand up, take her in my arms and kiss her eyelids. I don't, inhibited by some petty sense of shame.

Then, my dear, I set out to help her regain her good

humor. To get us out of our gloom, I deploy all my gifts as a clown. Naturally you are summoned up as part of this festival, along with your sister and her pharmacist, but I keep you in reserve for the finale.

I begin with Monsieur Tambourini. Tambourini is Lionel's manager. I tell Genevieve about the catastrophe of the curtains, which she grasps immediately, wonderful woman, and segue into the drama of the shutters, which you don't know about. I told you about the catastrophe of the curtains. In addition to the catastrophe of the curtains or I should say as companion piece to the catastrophe of the curtains, Lionel went through the drama of the shutters, refusing categorically that they be taken down to be repainted. To know the importance of *the window* in Lionel's life is to measure just how testing any instability in the life of objects can be to him. Lionel refuses to have his shutters taken down and sends for Tambourini. He immediately starts yelling, Monsieur TAMBOURINI, Monsieur TAMBOURINI, you want me to die! The literary critic in him rejects the violence of this introduction, You've killed my crescendo, he says to himself, but so what and he keeps going at the same pitch, you want to rob me of my shutters for a fortnight, my wife has just robbed me of my curtains to put up others which aren't yet lined which means they're not even there yet, which means that between you and my wife, Monsieur Tambourini, I have been reduced to a state in which I can no longer create in my own home the consolations of darkness, the CONSOLATIONS OF DARKNESS! Monsieur Tambourini, Monsieur Tambourini, I handed him his Tambourini, said Lionel, as I tell Genevieve to make her laugh, you understand a name like that, you can't make it up, Monsieur Tambourini, it's out of the question and stop trying to gargle with that expression Co-op Board, a Co-op Board is a collection of assholes and I don't belong to it and if they're assholes enough to pay 4,900 francs per window for a lick of white paint I'm glad for you all but don't count on me, Monsieur Tambourini, don't count on me to goosestep through the building! I'm yelling in the restaurant and Genevieve has found her smile again, I'm off to a good start. I move on to my vacation in Norway, to Serge Goulandri, our osteopath, whose gradually eroding positivism is a joy to us both, Lionel and me, as we finally watch the first glints of despair dawn over his view of life. During one of his sessions, Goulandri complains that he loses his sense of humor

when he's depressed. That's because you haven't hit
bottom, Lionel explains. Oh, okay, Goulandri says,
nodding profoundly. Genevieve laughs. I move on to
my illness, always an entertaining topic, I complain
about my stomach, I've ballooned right up, Genevieve,
I disgust myself, I complain about my stomach and
Michel my son-in-law (pharmacists think they're doc-
tors) says you eat too fast, that's why you've got a poor
digestion. In the *Tao-te-Ching,* interjects my daughter,
who's going further and further afield in search of
material to shore up the weightiness of her pronounce-
ments, the Taoists say you have to chew each mouthful
sixty times before you swallow. To which I reply they've
never been in Drancy, these guys.*

Genevieve is beaming beatifically and we crack
open a bottle of Nuits-Saint-Georges. After a quick
detour to Dacimiento, I get to you. My son, Genevieve, I start, my son . . . the *my son* comes out really
well, the tone is interrogative, which road should I
take, where should I begin? But my boy I don't go anywhere, I halt at the boundary of a subject I launched
into, admittedly, in a mischievous tone, I've barely said

*French transit camp for Auschwitz.

my son and a feeling of defeat sinks the jester in me, *my son* I say and I see, far away at the end of a corridor, a child bathed in yellow light, in a Zorro costume, sitting in front of an aquarium. You're not playing Zorro? I say to him. Papa, play the invincible one, you cry as you run toward me. No, I don't have time. Oh, please! I do two or three lunges as the invincible one. You wave your sword and try to get me. I dodge around the furniture in our apartment back then, thinking one day I won't be up to being the invincible one anymore, he'll catch me every time. Genevieve takes my arm: "Jean-Louis Hauvette!" she hisses in a whisper.

"Excuse me?"

"Behind you, there on the right, don't turn around, it's Jean-Louis Hauvette."

"Who's Jean-Louis Hauvette?"

"The man who killed Leo."

"Leo was assassinated?"

"In a manner of speaking."

"By this man?"

"Yes."

I turn around furtively and see the back of a man, sitting alone at a table by the window.

"Can you see his face in the glass?" says Genevieve in a whisper. "Samuel, be nice, stand up, walk past him, and get a discreet look at him."

"This man killed Leo?"

"He's responsible for his death."

"I'm going."

I go. I pretend to be going to the men's room and make a little detour to come back past the window. "I saw him."

"Old?"

"My age."

"Good-looking?"

"Ricardo Montalban after eighteen hours on the bus."

"That's him. Eyes?"

"Pale, from what I could see."

"It's him. Would someone recognize me, do you think? Have I changed a lot? We haven't seen each other for twenty years."

"Who was he?"

"My lover."

"Genevieve, I'm not following you at all, Genevieve."

"Jean-Louis Hauvette was the lover I took to save myself from Leopold," she says in a low voice, finishing what's in her glass. "I told you, Leo had no under-standing of the speed of life."

"And your husband?"

"What's he got to do with it?"

"You're making me dizzy, Genevieve."

"Abramowitz had nothing to do with any of this. My God, he can see me reflected in the glass. He doesn't recognize me. Women change more than men do."

"How did he kill Leo?"

"The two of us killed him together."

Genevieve falls silent. I wait. We sit for a moment without saying a word. "You amaze me," she says finally. "I would have thought you had more emanci-pated ideas."

"How horrible!" Again that exquisite laughter. "I admit," I say, "that I'm more inclined to accept your criminal behavior than your lovers."

"Same thing. I was quick to set aside my sentimen-tal tendencies. And I have never confused love and happiness. If I was unoccupied in my own home, I was unoccupied not the way a bored woman is unoccu-pied, but as a man waiting for a war to start that he's been preparing for. I don't know which Leo you knew, but the one I knew was a gambler and ravenous.

Desolation

Leopold Fench was war. I would, I think, have been an adversary on his own level if he'd shown himself more present on the battlefield. Don't look so lugubrious, my dear, I was trying on a style just to amuse you! There's only one truly sad thing in all this, and it's that I can talk about it all with such indifference. I would have preferred to be inconsolable. I trust people who are inconsolable, they're the only ones who reassure me about eternity."

"You're inconsolable, Genevieve."

"Ah? . . . maybe. Hauvette," she says, after another silence, taking a quick glance at the window, "Hauvette was nothing. The important thing in my liaison with this man was that Leo should hear about it. Hauvette in and of himself was nonexistent. The daughter of a mutual friend was getting married. Leo was supposed to come with his wife. Paul Abramowitz was chasing wild salmon in Canada (I had settled the Hauvette question with Abramowitz, made all the easier by the fact that he knew him and thought he was homosexual). I knew that the Fenches would be arriving late because Leo was coming back from the country. My plan was simple and good. To show myself with Hauvette during the first part of the evening and then disappear under some pretext or other before they arrived. You're interested in these women's stories," she says suddenly. "Frankly Samuel, you disappoint me."

"I'm interested in you, in Leo, in the unreality we were talking about and our return to nothingness."

"Good, good, good, I'll go on. I'll go on," she said. "Nothing went the way it was planned. The party was in a reception room at the Square du Temple. Instead of arriving late with his wife, Leo arrived early and alone, and without me seeing him come in. He surfaced in front of me, glass in hand, like someone who's been there some time already (I had been taking care to cling particularly assiduously to Hauvette's arm in front of any witnesses who might be liable to say to Leo, 'We've seen Genevieve'). I said, 'Leo.' He said, 'Good evening, Genevieve.' He inspected Hauvette and he said, 'Monsieur,' with a nod of the head. At that moment the orchestra struck up 'Hava Naguila,' the bridal couple went up onto the platform, everyone applauded them, Leo more warmly than anyone, it seemed to me, and he did something unimaginable to anyone who knew him, he took the hand of a woman, dragged her onto the dance floor, and opened the ball, you might say, in a whirling frenzy, glass in hand, right alongside the bride and groom. Leo, who was the opposite of the life and soul of any party, Leo, whose fantasy and daring had nothing to do with exuberance. This ghastly atmosphere of joy and shared emotion immediately built up and enveloped all the guests, led by Hauvette. At a certain point, I lost sight of Leo. I told Hauvette I wasn't feeling well, which was absolutely true. I hunted for Leo around the room, someone told me they'd seen him leave, I ran to the cloakroom, there were people arriving and others leaving, I handed my purse to Hauvette, who was following right on my heels like an idiot, I said there's someone I must speak to, and I hurried outside, half-naked, in mid-winter, no coat, no scarf, nothing. At first I didn't see him. I started to run in one direction, I had to choose one, I took this street and that, at random, finally where I could see some parked cars I came to a street called rue Charlot, I stopped and I called his name. Farther along this rue Charlot a man halted and I recognized Leo. What is the use of intelligence, Samuel? We are so defenseless in the face of life. 'Calm down, Genevieve, catch your breath,' said Leo, opening his car door. 'It's all for the best. In some kind of attack of sudden impulse, I'd decided in fact to spend the evening and perhaps the night with you' (we'd never stayed together a whole night). 'Thank God your fickle behavior came at exactly the right moment to put an end to such a stupid plan.' I'm paraphrasing to give you the essence of what he said, Samuel," says Genevieve, "his words were chosen with such nonchalant cruelty that I can barely reproduce their power to wound. 'Everything is for the best, my dear. What years of hesitations and agonizing doubts couldn't bring me to do, you have achieved with decisive grace and the lightest of touches. You've finally set me free, Genevieve. And I must admit something to you: while it would have been almost impossible for me to get there on my own, I sincerely envy the ease, the flick of the wrist, with which you eliminated me. Oh, but look who's coming, look who's running with all your bits and pieces! Such sedulous devotion, Genevieve, fantastic! Quick, warm her up, Monsieur, she's shivering, make her as warm as you can, Monsieur, Monsieur . . . ?' 'Hauvette,' said Hauvette. 'Monsieur Ôvette,' said Leo, getting into his car, 'take good care of Madame Abramowitz.' 'What's going on?' asked Hauvette, seeing that I looked stricken. You know, Samuel, what we call courage, pugnacity, are words born of our pride in order to disguise our helplessness when confronted with our fate. 'Did he do something to offend you?' he added grotesquely. 'He's just wonderful!' Leo laughed. 'Monsieur Ôvette, please be good enough to let go of the door, I would like to drive off.' 'I don't like your tone, Monsieur—' 'Fench,' said Leo. 'I don't give a shit what your name is,' snapped Hauvette, 'I don't give a shit who you are, I don't like your tone and I don't like your effect on Genevieve.' 'Monsieur Ôvette,' said Leo, whose restraint was fraying, 'if you enjoy indulging in the kind of appalling complication commonly known as an affair, I recommend Madame Abramowitz, I most highly recommend Madame Abramowitz,' said Leo, who was getting worked up and since Hauvette wouldn't let go of the car door, he got out of the car again. 'Madame Abramowitz,' said Leo, eyeing Hauvette up and down or rather down and up because Hauvette parenthetically was a good head taller than he was, 'is docile, shy, affectionate, and quick to treachery, she possesses the whole little bag of tricks of contradictory qualities that ensnare you by your basest instincts, one would praise a good household pet, please note, no differently.' 'Genevieve, would you like me to intervene?' said Hauvette, rising in revolt. 'Madame Abramowitz likes authoritarian men, my friend, feel free to intervene without asking her permission.' 'Shut your face!' yelled Hauvette in a sudden fit of incivility, seizing a windshield wiper he'd literally yanked off the windshield. And then, I hardly dare tell you this bit," said Genevieve, "as if this weren't enough to finish us off, he started trying to threaten Leo with this ridiculous stick (the rubber bit was hanging down off it) and hissing hysterically 'Get the hell out, get the hell out.' 'You know, you got yourself a real daredevil here!' sneered Leo. 'One more word to Madame Abramowitz and I'll slash you,' yelled Hauvette, pointing his weapon. At that point Leo lost it and with one violent blow he flattened Hauvette's arm, the windshield wiper, and Hauvette, who crumpled onto the hood. Then he got back into the car, put it in gear before Hauvette had time to get up again, rolled down the window, and yelled, 'Beat it, you piece of shit,' and to me, pointing to him, 'Bravo, Genevieve, *first class!*' He roared off and I never saw him again. Two days later he was dead."

We clink glasses in silence. And in silence she and I contemplate, I by dint of twisting around so that I can see him reflected in the glass, the remains of Jean-Louis Hauvette, murderer of Leopold Fench.

The remains don't amount to much, if truth be told, but then what would remain of an old man sitting alone at a table on Place des Ternes, watching the shadows of passing traffic behind a window?

"Were you angry at him?"

"Terribly."

"Until this evening?"

"No, not anymore, this evening," she murmurs, stricken.

We agree that pity has a catastrophic effect on all forms of vitality.

By hating him unflinchingly (and Hauvette was all the more to be hated because unjustly accused), Genevieve had kept Hauvette in focus. She had saved him from old age and oblivion. For as long as anger and resentment lasted, their pitiful story endured too. A slightly hunched back, a general air of solitude, and Genevieve was undone. Everything was undone. Because the only reality is subjective. Enter pity, and Genevieve, Hauvette, and even Leo had all reverted to insignificance. Enter pity and the eroding effects of time (are they the same thing? yes) and the episode in the rue Charlot and the death that followed, and the life that followed, are no more than minute, infinitesimally minute dislocations.

Disturb God.

Take a little step back so that He can enter the world, every day, and several times a day, and your whole life long.

I cannot boast of having taken it. That little step. Not even for a single day. Not even once, I'm ashamed to say, my boy, without expecting a response, without hoping for a hearing. The Jew, the real Jew, says to God, I have obeyed You, come, I've made room for you in our world, and I ask nothing, absolutely nothing, from you.

Disturb God. This, yes, this I have done. But you see there are no laws that govern this enterprise. And life, my boy, doesn't like being disturbed. Mankind aspires to comfort. To disturb life is to take the road of genuine desperation.

"Genevieve, everything beyond the immediate moment is unreal. Soon all three of us will be dead and buried. Let's invite Jean-Louis Hauvette to join us."

Desolation

"How do I look?"

"Beautiful."

"Old?"

"No."

"So go."

Jean-Louis Hauvette is finishing a sole. I say, excuse me, and I tell him that a woman he hasn't seen for a long time would like to speak to him. He listens to me and turns round toward Genevieve. Then something happens that is totally unforeseen. Genevieve looks up in my direction, makes a gesture I don't understand, and starts to laugh, laugh uncontrollably, into her napkin. Jean-Louis Hauvette looks at her for a moment and turns back to me. "Who is it?" he asks.

"Genevieve Abramowitz," I say.

"I'm glad I amuse this person. I have no idea who she is," he says, sticking a fork into his last potato.

"But you are Jean-Louis Hauvette, aren't you?" I try stupidly.

"Not at all," he says, dismissing me.

My son—what should I have said?

Are you going to go on and on fucking around like this? A little thrill in Malaysia, a little dose of culture in

Jordan, then three months off with more people who like to fuck around in the Luberon. The world is within reach of absolutely anybody these days. And everything is familiar, everything is overrun. Not one place left *untouched*. I finally have a certain sympathy for the Afghans and all religious fanatics in general. You're not going to go visiting them, at least. Whole herds of you aren't going to go trash the slopes of Pamir.

My son.

Did you open the fridge? Have you taken in the sad sight of the fridge? Here or in the rue Ampère, same fridge, same sad sight. Nancy doesn't give a damn, she's above these trivialities, and Dacimiento never buys what I like. When I open the fridge now, what do I see? Caramel puddings, cream cheese with fruit, and yogurt drinks. For Jerome, obviously. Jerome, who's here three times a month, sets the rules in my fridge. Jerome is apparently a particularly precocious child. At the age of two and a half, he can make rhymes. The other day your sister said "bread and butter, see," . . . "pretty face on me" was Jerome's immediate response. General bedazzlement. In which I joined. I'm not an expert, maybe it is extraordinary, age two and a half, to say pretty face on me when someone says bread and butter, see. In any case, he's a coddled, loved, and praised little creature, and he's off to a good start, as far as I can make out. You, my poor boy, you never had any Pop Tarts or Dannon yogurts (the brand names stick in my brain the moment I close the fridge), I don't remember your very first efforts at poetry and if I loved you, I certainly didn't build an altar to your status as a child. Nancy's and your mother's version: I traumatized you. The examples they quote me are ridiculous. One day—one episode among others—your mother and I went to see your teacher, you were beginning to read and write. The teacher was satisfied: I'm pleased, she said, he's become socialized this year; last year he didn't join in the other children's games, he stayed in his own world and asked questions that are not appropriate at that age. Your mother and the teacher congratulated themselves on this happy development, and instead of joining in, I gave you the cold shoulder (a child of five!) because I was incapable of being pleased that you were mixing with other children and becoming part of the herd. Another story about school, from later on, you came home from high school with the results of a math test. You had come fifth and you were over the moon at coming fifth (you were usually second from the bottom). Instead of promising you a model Spitfire, I apparently said to you in a disappointed voice, "And why not first?" Upon which you burst into tears, ran into your room, and slammed the door howling, "You're never satisfied, you're so mean!" Jerome will certainly be able to tell his father he's so mean without causing the least upset. In my day, nobody talked to his father like that. I went straight into your room and gave you a hiding.

The funny part of it is that instead of hardening you up, I produced a weakling. And I didn't even make an enemy of you. If only you were my enemy, at least! In the spineless perversity of your inertia, I detect indifference, even a whiff of condescension. If I was wrong, I've certainly been punished for it. I've created a perfect stranger.

Nancy, who likes to sing your praises—if you go in for generosity, the conciliating stepmother is a favorite tune to play—had this curious thing to say: "One accepts things from one's children one wouldn't accept from anyone else." "How do you mean, my love" (I'm as gentle as a lamb with Nancy from now on), "is that a victory or a surrender?" "Neither one nor the other," she said, exasperated, "it's just a fact." I have never argued with Nancy. During the blessed time when she was depressed, I used to take her indifference for agreement and since she started priding herself on being able to cross swords with me intellectually, I keep my mouth shut. So you are going to be the first to savor the answer I didn't give her. Children, Nancy, I could have said to her if time's abrading passage hadn't separated us as much as it has, children, my dear little Nancy, are the lowest rung on the ladder of human desires. If we conceive them, we do so at least in the hope of having *someone to talk to* at the end of our lives. I am already in the process, Nancy, of accepting my old age and the defeat of my body. I accept that I've lost the game of life in the same way that one loses at solitaire, I accept that, just as I accept these days that things are slowing down, I can even accept that there's nothing going on, provided my body holds out a little longer, I accept that my light is slowly going out and I accept the ordinary death that will step into my place. I am in the process, Nancy, of accepting how modest a chapter in time mine has been.

So on top of all this, my love, must I also adapt

myself to the inanity of my descendants? Under the
pretext that these are my genes, must I forgive someone whose views of the world make me sick to my
stomach? In a word, must I accept—the very thought
makes me shiver—that the final person in my life is a
worm whose ideal is not to get in a fight with anyone?
In my philosophy, Nancy, I would have said to her, a
father wants his son not to be like the rest of humanity.
In my philosophy, what is good for everyone else is not
good for my son. I couldn't give a fuck, I would have
said to Nancy, though she wouldn't have allowed me
to go that far, I don't give a fuck, please understand,
that this boy spends his time flocking from Java to
Bermuda and back again, and if I keep coming back to
this more than is necessary, it's because every mention
of this ludicrous geography feeds my sense of mockery.
But I don't give a fuck how he lives his life, I don't give
a fuck if he's in this place or that, whether he's doing
this or that is a matter of total indifference to me, I
don't give a fuck if his mediocrity is, in society's view,
more or less acceptable. Whatever he does and wher-
ever he goes, whether he elbowed his way in or trum-
peted his lack of ambition, my son has *adapted* to the
modern world. I have sired a *well-adapted man* (read:

adapted to everyone except his father). I have given life to someone who, like a mutating fly—I read in *Science and the Future* that a breed of flies that got trapped in the London Underground while it was being built mutated a hundred times faster than normal in order to survive—ends up bowing to the exigencies of the world, sees what's reasonable and makes himself at home there, finds a comfortable little niche or two and settles in to wait for his own extinction. When you were a teenager, my boy, you had a sort of attack of nerves, an obsession with revenge, something set fire to you. I approved of that son. He was hostile to me, but I recognized him. You defied me with that ridiculous thirst for the absolute that everyone has at that age and I said to myself, The boy is as obstreperous as one could hope for, he's going to manage to break out. But you didn't break out of anything. Once the upheavals of youth were over, you went back to your place in the ranks of the average. No more trace of rebellion. No more trace of revenge. No more trace of passion. Everything that nourishes a man and fortifies him and lifts him out of the conditions of his existence, you consigned to oblivion. You traded fever for restraint. And you did it before you'd even set foot in inhospitable territory, before even daring to take a few steps into the kingdoms of uncertainty. You were so quick to fear for your own skin, my poor child. Like the rest of the troop of your wormlike friends, you know that every act has its price, and so from the beginning you chose never to stand out again. Avoiding suffering, that's your whole horizon. Avoiding suffering is your substitute for the heroic epic. Ladies and gentlemen, allow me to present my son, a cut flower from the gang of cut flowers. I would have liked you better as a criminal or a terrorist than as a militant in the cause of happiness.

I would have liked him better as a criminal than as a militant for happiness, I'd have said to Nancy if the solitude of marriage hadn't rendered any exchange pointless. "What dramatics!" she would have said and smiled as she stroked my face, if the collapse of our marriage hadn't rendered any caress impossible. My ideal man—let us admit right away he's not exactly common—my ideal man, Nancy, I would have gone on in the flush of tenderness, is the man who has chosen ferocity. He doesn't *adapt*, he doesn't deny the hatred that sustains and shapes him, he's not concerned with survival if it means he has to renounce himself like the English fly. He doesn't say yes to the world. He doesn't cower in his pathetic little hole like your mentor André Petit-Pautre, my love. Petit-Pautre comes home with an article about his book, his wife swallows his cock, and he believes that humanity is a great success. That's how people live. My son also believes that humanity is a great success. You only have to witness his little air of superiority when he comes home from visiting one of his small tribes. My ideal man doesn't give a fuck about being accepted by the Bambaras or the Talking Heads either. He doesn't want to be loved, he wants to conquer. He doesn't want to heal himself, he wants to win. My ideal man has the power to summon the dawn, would have been the climax of my peroration as I watched for the tears to spring to Nancy's eyes. But Nancy, who cries ten times a day over nothing, is immune to this flight of ideas.

All this reminds me of a recent conversation I had with Lionel. Lionel phones up, scandalized, because he's just discovered that in Jewish tradition life is accorded supreme value. "*You must choose life,*" he intones disgustedly, "Deuteronomy, last Book of Moses. What's all this stuff about you must choose life?

Explain this humiliation!" As I'm stumbling my way through a commentary on the nonliteralness of the commandment (I'm always equipped with some driveling half-assed positive explanation for every Jewish saying), Lionel bellows down the receiver, "Long live the Greeks!"

Making any such speech to Nancy would have undone me. He who reviles his fellowmen is soon undone, because what he wishes to make understood is quite simply *beyond words.*

We are alone. My child. Our solitude is immense. Total. And there is virtually no link between one solitude and another. Solitude is long. The joys that connect us leave almost no trace.

Every day the world shrivels me and today, it is the world inside me that has shriveled. That is how things are. In the end, I will have been vanquished by life. As it vanquished Leopold Fench. As it vanquishes all who desire it intensely. Nothing can reach the peak of our desires, my child. Except solitude. My entire life has slipped past between these two words. These words draw the arc of my little interval in time. God has withdrawn, it seems, in order to create a space that was not

Desolation

His before. God, who was All, to whom lack was foreign, had the catastrophic idea of withdrawing so that others (another concept that was foreign to Him) could experiment with this curse. On the question of life's inadequacy, Arthur (astonishing how everything about him is coming back to me all of a sudden) once accused me of lacking humility. Look, he argued, look at the Einsteins, the Lubitsches, the Bruno Walters, etc. And on went the list of names, some familiar, some not, of people who were more or less exiles, more or less storm-tossed by history or life, whose joie de vivre, optimism, and lack of self-pity were supposed to teach me a lesson. To which I would have liked to present my own opposing list, forged in the same adversity but a little less frisky, but my unfamiliarity with the cultural world meant that no names leapt to mind (nowadays I have a list that gets added to every day, and would floor him).

Lack of humility. It's possible. But why should I be humble? Humble before what, before whom?

Accept whatever life offers us that is good, said the idiot. And what has it offered me, you cretin, that I didn't seize for myself? The only reality, Arthur, lies wrapped in my desires. The world doesn't make offerings.

Lionel told me yesterday morning that he'd finally hit bottom. Task for the day, I had told him: fight despair. "Oh, you're still stuck back there," he sighs: "you plan and you fight. I, finally, thank God, have reached bottom."

Note the peculiarity. Lionel, my friend and the most passionate of men, is on a relentless search for the absence of passion. What causes my suffering, my boy, is what I see in your look. A look that alternates between pity and boredom. And maybe also irritation. You listen to me, you force yourself to be here and nothing you hear gets inside you, nothing speaks to you, nothing touches you. Do you know that another person's empty presence is the greatest lack of all? Have you ever felt that? Even when you think you're being heard and being loved, the other person persists in being absent. And yours, my child, is extreme. I can take your hand, and yet you couldn't be farther away. We are incapable of taking the smallest step together.

Desolation

In your eyes I read your utter incomprehension and my own old age. I read my abandonment. I read a confirmation of my solitude.

Making any such speech to Nancy would have undone me.

Why so excessive, why so ungentle and unforbearing? —Yes, Nancy, I'm so sorry. —So why? —I have to be in balance with myself. —In balance with yourself, that means really working to be sarcastic and showing that you're inhuman? —Apparently. —What self-satisfaction! —My love, to start posing as well balanced, I'd need rather more of a future than I've got. I'm no longer driven by the longing to build up any particular product of my own vanity, including my own persona. I am too close to my own disintegration to get involved with nuances. Before I end up on a public bench with my friends the zombies, allow me, my generous friend, to sing the praises of intolerance, the elect, and general injustice. Grant me immoderation, the only way to save what we can of what we're given. The hell with equity. Your friend Dacimiento wrecked the cooktop on the Aga in less than a year. Ask her what on earth she used to plane down the controls.

No justice. The problem with this woman is that you could park a dead donkey on a shelf in front of her and she wouldn't see it. I put in a kitchen for her that cost $2,700, and instead of lighting up with joy every morning when she sees it again and running around waving her arms, she puts on the kind of martyred look that explains every single summary execution in history. All of it just because on the thirtieth of November at eight in the morning, the light doesn't come sparkling down on her in the rue Ampère the way she'd like. No justice.

The garden—all me.

I've done it all according to my own whims. Every which way. I didn't start with flowers right away, I did the trees first, then the vegetables, then one day I put in the lawn, with my left hand, so to speak. The moment I left, the lawn turned into a prairie. Lawns take maintenance, they take mowing, they take watering. Who knew? Finally, what do you want, I bought some books. Too much money out the window, too many mistakes. Today you've seen the azaleas, the rhododendrons, the roses (four varieties). The Fortunys came two weeks ago. René and his wife Jeanne.

Desolation

Dazzled. I showed them my collection of clippers, if you want I'll show them to you too. Do you? I've got about twenty. I keep thinking I'm going to find a better pair. An even finer blade, that will cut even more cleanly. Sometimes I go back to the old ones. I have my favorites. Even when they're worn out, I keep them. I'm attached to every one of them. The Fortunys were interested in my tools, in the spades, in the sprayers — I'm nuts about sprayers — they were interested in my problems with amending the soil, and watering systems, and making new borders. It was cold and gray that day, and they walked around the garden, stopping in front of the flowerbeds, the trees, the walls, I watched them from the summerhouse and I thought what are you complaining about, this is what friends are.

At a certain point, René gestured — I can't talk about it without feeling a pang — he bent down, picked up an armful of dead leaves, and threw them over Jeanne. She laughed and protested and chased him round the oak tree to give him a smack. There was one leaf that stayed stuck to her woolen cap, like a pompom. She was running around the tree, all awkward in her little boots, they were both running around in circles, laughing, René started clowning back around in the opposite direction, she stopped to catch her breath against the tree trunk and he caught her gloved hand and kissed it.

Arthur has never understood how I could say, René has no taste. He has never understood how I can say, Have you seen that hideous living room? I couldn't remain friends with someone who cannot grasp that talking about the hideousness of René's living room like that is an act of tenderness, that recognizing the hideousness of the Fortunys' living room to be exceptional, definitive, grandiose even, is the mark of real affection.

This little race around the oak tree under a gray sky (finally I love low, gray skies most of all), this little kiss on her gloved fingers, redoubled my affection for Jeanne and René Fortuny.

For forty years from his window Lionel has been watching the metamorphoses of a tree. Every day, season by season. The bare branches, the first leaves, summer, fall. Everything that's still green, still beautiful, normal-sized, he says, is down underneath, away from

the light. Up at the ends, patches of faded ocher, brit-
tleness, ragged remains.

I spend half my life amongst trees and greenery, I
don't see what Lionel sees. An object has to be unique,
alone, to be visible. The nest has disappeared this year,
he said.

*Capriccio sopra la lontananza del suo fratello dilettis-
simo.* A little work by Bach (little as regards length) discovered thanks to Serkin, via Lionel. The two of us
sang the *adagiosissimo* on the phone this morning, the
"Friends' Lamento":

> *Fa mi mi re' re' do   sigh   tee do tee tee*
> *La la soh fa fa mi mi   sigh*

Lionel told me that after he woke up and listened to
this song, he felt it would be idiotic to plan any other
experiences for the day. The repeated notes, the
silences, the interruptions cut through him and justi-
fied his paralysis.

According to Bach specialists, it's a pleasant little
youthful composition—with a hint of irony in it.
Experts flatten the world.

. . .

Marisa Botton is sixty today.

One day I stuck a Toblerone in her vagina and we ate it afterward. A Toblerone she'd bought for her son. At the beginning, she wouldn't even drink a glass of anything with me. "In Rouen, one doesn't drink with a stranger."

"I'm not a stranger."

"You're worse, you're one of my husband's suppliers."

"All right, then, I have no chance of seeing you anywhere except this corridor."

"No."

I knew this meant yes.

At that time telephones were not in such wide use as they are today. You couldn't reach people directly at their desks, you had to go through the switchboard. I called myself Monsieur Ostinato, an improvised name I borrowed from musical terminology. Who was Monsieur Ostinato? Even after clearing the switchboard you weren't certain you'd get through to her and you had to tell the inquisitorial voice the purpose of your call. Monsieur Ostinato was a contractor and wanted to give her a private estimate on something. Monsieur Ostinato was only pressed into service once (Marisa thought it was the world's worst idea, at Aunay's everyone knew everything, and all it would take was the slightest thing and someone would start asking her husband about the improvements they were having made to their house) but seduced her with his boldness and his wild imagination. Monsieur Ostinato got his rendezvous one April evening at six o'clock in the bar of the Hotel de Dieppe.

She came a quarter of an hour late, a little disappointing in a pale raincoat.

It took me six months to have her. After Ostinato there were other names, other tricks, other lightning rendezvous at the station, at the Bar de la Poste, at the Bar du Palais, at the Dieppe, at the Scotch, the bar in the basement of the Hotel d'Angleterre, she came wearing glasses, she stayed for five minutes with her eyes fixed on the door, she said we can't see each other anymore, you must forget me, she said in my ear I want you, whenever I think about you I can't sleep, she just couldn't do it, she could never do it, there was her son, her husband, her mother, the factory, Rouen, the universe, there was no place to go, there was no time, I was going mad.

One day, I had her. At lunchtime, in a room at the Hotel de la Poste, on the rue Jeanne-d'Arc.

Disturbing life.

There you are, sitting in a good restaurant, you've ordered a good wine, you're trying to hustle a hundred thousand pairs of pajamas, you're having a pro forma argument but the client isn't even really using the conditional tense, you can sense it's gone well, you talk golf or some such bullshit, you laugh with the client till the teeth fall out of your head, which incidentally you've always said I was naturally incapable of, you laugh, the buyer leans forward, you clink glasses, you show him your honest face while you calculate your margin, and instead of being no, not happy, heaven forfend, not even satisfied, but just you, pure and simple, you're fucked, annihilated, you're shivering in the yawning void that separates you from Marisa, aka Christine Botton, in charge of planning and contract administration at Aunay-Foulquier.

Why didn't things stay as they were at that point? Two little hours in the rue Jeanne-d'Arc. Two sort-ofmongrel-hours of no particular rapture or even the sweetness of beginnings. But how can we give up our own imaginations, and if we did, where would we be headed? She suited me because she was so out of whack, she said yes, she said no, and yes and no at the same time, she suited me because I didn't understand her . . . you see, my boy, even today I'm inventing her all over again . . . she suited me because I never wearied of desiring her, because she was an illusion that kept *receding*, and I would rise to that like a fish to the ultimate bait.

One evening, the last (the last evening of a folly that lasted almost three years and incidentally caused me to split up with your mother), I was waiting for her in a room at the Dieppe (waiting would be my definition of it). Botton was at Interstoff, the annual textiles fair in Frankfurt. Her son was supposedly at her sister's. I waited, swallowing packages of potato crisps I'd stolen from the deserted bar, washed down with tap water (back then there were no minibars and no televisions in the rooms), reread the Paris-Normandy newspaper for the forty-sixth time, paced around like a deranged person banging into the furniture, at two in the morning I called her house. She picked up sounding fast asleep, her voice just killed me. I said, I'm leaving the hotel and I'm coming over. She said, No, no, don't do that, you know you can't. I yelled, Here's what I know, I've been waiting for you for four hours in this nightmare of a room. She whispered, My son has a fever, I kept him at home. I knew she was lying, I said, Me too, me too, I've got a fever, she laughed and hung up. I called back, I yelled, You'll never see me again, you're nothing but a little provincial slut, you're not even beautiful, you're NOTHING. I went back to Paris that same night in a state of genuine collapse.

Next morning, I was on my way to the office and this guy on the boulevard des Capucines handed me a tract for Aid to the Sahara or something. *There's no greater suffering,* it said on the piece of paper, *than that of a mother who has to watch helplessly as her child dies.* I thought, what do you know, asshole, and I crumpled the flyer. Because what was in danger of being extinguished that day wasn't love or any form of earthly attachment but the very illusion of life. It doesn't matter, my boy, that this illusion was limited to the corridors at Aunay's, hotel-room walls, car seats, and the occasional miserable gateway in Rouen, i.e., nothing that could possibly bear a close or a distant resemblance to the ordinary run of life's illusions. There was never the faintest atmosphere of romance between us, not a single place we visited together, no wood where we walked, not a single landscape, no unfamiliar street, no place in the world we ever took the time to just be. We never did more than pause on thresholds, halt in ephemeral stairwells, and if I had the faintest talent at analyzing things, I'd conclude that with Marisa the illusion of life was all the more violent because it was unadorned by any external element whatever, and never, never confused with happiness.

With your brother-in-law Michel I can have conversations about constipation. I mean to say I can have scientific conversations with him. With Arthur, back then, I could also have such conversations, but they were man-to-man, or rather, one damned man to another. With Michel there's some hope mixed in. I have to say to his credit that the boy does seem to know his digestive tract. For starters, he calls it the "transit," which is a nice touch. Last Sunday, he switched me from Duphalac to Transipeg, which is supposed to be less bloating. Duphalac worked for me, but made me bloated. He forbids me to use glycerine suppositories. Obviously I'm not going to pay any attention. If I listened to him, I'd use those Eductyl suppositories of his, you shit water every ten minutes four times in a row. Michel never comes to see me without a whole little suitcase of medicines. He knows all my illnesses, he's interested, and he enjoys fine-tuning my treatments. Your sister, who has developed something of an ecological bent, disapproves, of course. Michel is a good pharmacist, maybe even an excellent pharmacist, and I'd be glad to see him often if our exchanges were confined to the riveting sphere of illnesses and their cures. But how are you supposed to put out the welcome mat for someone who's just spent the morning jogging from Montfort to Coignières and working his way back by train on the B line with his friends the Jewish Ramblers, without ever mentioning the subject, without asking him for example what secret branch of the tradition produced these lunatics. He takes it badly. A nice boy all the same, happy to help with the weeding, always interested in my health. Threaten his Jewish integrity (his exact words), and within three minutes flat—it never fails—he'll be invoking genocide as a way of calling me to order. And reminding me that solidarity is not a metaphor. That it's not necessary to go all the way back to the Garden of Eden to hold out a hand to someone, that if you want to remake the world you have to cut through the everyday games. To remind me that we are still these poor little birds stripped of our feathers, and our urgent task, if we are ever to recover our cohesion and our dignity, is to fly toward one another until we meet, be it in Jerusalem or Coignières, because Michel Cukiermann's tribe is no longer the People of the Book, but the People of the Shoah. So, because he patiently explained Transipeg to me in all its technical detail, I do not say to him that *my* people, be they the People of the Book, the People of Pride, or the People of Solitude, are bitter and untrained in a different way, that to my knowledge they have never compared themselves to a shivering brood of baby birds, and I do not say that my own suffering is one it is much harder to admit to, namely, that I am forced to confront him in all his pathetic gravity, his righteousness and brotherhood, without *disemboweling* him.

My son, I cannot, absolutely cannot, speak one more word to anyone who lacks the capacity for doubt, who has cocooned himself in everyday simplifications, who sets up against me his own edifying vision of the world. You have certainly avoided such rigidities and you don't act out such passions, but you have dismissed any form of ambition, opting instead for the complete pointlessness of doing anything. My friend Lionel also represents a vote for humanity as inertia, but you're not in the same camp. Lionel doesn't expect anything. Lionel looks at the sheer pointlessness of the day-to-day and he takes evasive action. You, my dear, are still nursing your own little pet project, because what you want is to blossom. Since I've been taking a close interest in plants and flowers, this expression has taken on real meaning. You lift your arms in a corolla, you offer your head to the passing breeze, and you beam at anyone who walks by.

Certain pieces in *The Art of the Fugue* have the wherewithal to make my soul dance. First Fugue, Counterpoint 1, slow, fast, never wearied of listening to it, stated, restated, never wearying, slow, fast, slow, listening for hours, my boy, sometimes slower, sometimes faster, all of life playing itself out uninterruptedly in one's ear, never wearying, Counterpoint 10, Counterpoint 12, Counterpoint 13, the thirteenth fugue! danced, sung at the hardest of moments, ineffable dance, ineffable song, bearer of ineffable joy, Counterpoint 14, *unfinished* as per the record sleeve, I liked the word *unfinished*, mi, re', do, tee, lah, tee, re'—STOP—interruption caused by death, long radical silence, the work isn't uncompleted, it's infinite, it's not incomplete but *unfinished*, arrested, rendered infinite by the grave.

Bach will save me from you all, from your revolting versions of paradise, Bach will save my life.

"My current wife, Nancy," I say to Genevieve, "is capable of standing motionless—you could time her—in a discount drugstore for an hour at a stretch choosing *loose* face powder (I still don't know what that is)."

"Doesn't seem abnormal to me," says Genevieve.

"No, not at all abnormal, on the contrary I was expressing regret."

"She doesn't do it anymore?"

"These days Nancy, although she's beautiful to me, spends her money on rejuvenating creams and potions, but, how can I put it, her bent is now scientific. No more of that charming tendency to err toward the magical. Sooner or later women abandon futility."

"That's what you think. No more than two weeks ago—and Samuel, I'm no longer in the bloom of youth—I threw a tantrum because I couldn't get my usual lipstick. I said Arancil is no longer making Bamboo? I said, they've *discontinued* Bamboo?! I'm talking too loud, aren't I? Samuel, I'm pissed, you've got me completely drunk, my friend, you know I basically don't drink. Our friend the false Hauvette is leaving. He's not so terrible. The real Hauvette is probably not that well preserved. He may even be dead. At our age, there's a good chance we're dead, no? It's our only rendezvous these days. Which is why I'm capable of going all the way across Paris for a lipstick or a lightning face-firming gel, the hell with the gravity of our final moments, I want pure fantasy, because waiting at the end of the road, my dear, what's waiting is Bagneux where I'll be stuck with Abramowitz and his parents, who were already dead as doornails while they were alive, when I would have been so happy to be in Montparnasse in the Jewish part of the cemetery next to Leopold, finally sleeping next to him, even as dust, even in oblivion, even as nothing. Finally no more having to get up and pretend to take everything so lightly, no more standing forever on the threshold of my own life, a little mocking, a little unreliable, a little treacherous, no more wasting my physical strength and my time fighting against the love I felt for him, you're pouring me another glass, you must take total responsibility for the state I'm in, Montparnasse is still part of the city, you go walking there without thinking twice, you take the children and hunt for entertaining figures among the dead, Leo would have hated being at Bagneux, last time I laid a pebble on his grave, almost a year ago, it was already dark, and I forbid you to laugh, we talked to each other: where were you all our lives? I murmured, when my life intersected with yours, where were you, now I'm too old to attract you, love passes me by and doesn't even see me. —This is what I wanted, Genevieve. —What did you want? —That your face would be soft. That time would have left its marks, that I can stroke it the way you stroke a dog. —Why? He doesn't answer. I ask why, but he doesn't answer. There's nothing more than the brown gravestone and the pebble in one corner, just as I too, during his life, stayed in a corner, and, absurdly, I tell them all the things I would never ever have said out loud while he was alive, I tell the marble and the incised letters things I left unsaid while my life and his intersected, and that will still remain unsaid tonight, even though I'm lightheaded, because I will never worry again about upsetting him or contradicting him or losing him, death has given him to me. Help, Samuel, right away, we have to get some fresh air."

Stand up, Genevieve, I said, in the living room in rue Ampère, where we found ourselves after walking the whole length of the Park Monceau and sitting for quite some while in the rotunda. Stand up, Genevieve, I commanded after we'd shared a third of a surviving bottle of vodka. Stand up, come on, we'll move the armchairs, let's push back the chairs and the table, I'll close the curtains, Genevieve, and make rue Ampère and Paris and time all disappear, give me your hand and we'll dance, *Jewish Songs for Cello and Piano,* present from my son-in-law Michel, never listened to them before, it's just like opening a bottle of some ancient nectar with you but I think we've drunk enough, let's dance instead, this evening we'll dance to *Uncertainty* and the *Kaddish* and the *Kol Nidre,* I was born somewhere between Samara and Kazan on the Volga, somewhere between deserted roads and deserted villages, I'm going to die in the bed in that bedroom next door, a good bed to croak in, as I said to Nancy the other day, she was lying on the daybed for once in her life as was I, I said it's perfect for keeping watch over someone who's dying, you smile, Nancy, but that's where you'll be, in the armchair, I mean, my love, I'll be in the bed. Frankly I don't know which is the better spot. Let's dance, Genevieve, the steppes are blanketed in white, there are no walls and no doors, the road we're traveling doesn't matter anymore. The little pre-Columbian goat has lost a leg, Rosa Dacimiento threw it out, a little leg made of clay, what does she think she's doing? In the great tradition of Audoulia, I run the cloth over the bookcase slowly to begin with, then speed up as I get closer to the clay statue, laugh, Genevieve, laugh, I do so love your laugh, I'll do the impossible, go anywhere, if it'll make you laugh. Audoulia was our pre-Dacimiento, Spanish, my boy as a mere child made model fighter planes, and she broke them all dusting, she didn't dust, she dueled with fighter squadrons, I miss her today, just as I miss everything to do with times past, whether it's Audoulia, a leather bag, or the smell of fresh-sawn lumber, I'm immensely nostalgic, Genevieve, incurably nostalgic, it's something that can wreck your reputation in a minute these days, if you're nostalgic you're one of our world's bastards, I hate our world. Nancy is in Brest, at her parents'. My wife Nancy, Genevieve, is forging right ahead, and since she's been forging right ahead she's no longer pretending to jump out of the window, she no longer rolls around on the ground, she beats me periodically and that makes me feel a rediscovered tenderness for her because this madness makes me remember her old fragility, I used to love Nancy, I loved her fits, I loved her laugh, she had the laugh I love, your laugh, and Lionel's. Arthur's before he became the universal man. She called me at the office to say I'm off to kill myself, do you realize this is the last time you'll hear me on the phone, I said but where are you, she started to cry, I'm stuck in traffic on the avenue de la Grande Armée, even when I need to kill myself I can't get out of Paris. That was the Nancy I loved. I went to get her, I took her shopping, she spent a century choosing a face powder or a pair of shoes, she gave it the same sincerity, the same serious-ness she had brought an hour before to the idea of killing herself, I waited for her in overheated rooms, sitting on makeshift stools, we came out clutching parcels, she hung on my neck and kissed me, half-laughing, half-crying, and I ended up crying with her and we both cried over how hard life is and the price of shoes, why our paths are diverging like this, why she's become this socially engaged person, driven from dawn to dusk by the world as adventure, once she didn't give a shit, now that she's in love with illegal aliens from Mali she's no longer in love with me, since she's come down on the side of generosity, she's out to kill me. Let's dance. What we're listening to is a *Prayer*. Let's dance, Genevieve, before us there was nobody and after us there will be nobody. The world goes on, but for nothing. Let's dance. I was born in a country that existed in a different time, on white plains, I am incurably nostalgic for empty villages, empty roads, empty sounds, how am I supposed to follow my wife in all her humanistic bustle? I'm happy to go back into winter where I came from. Maybe that's the distant place that gave me my taste for gray light and it's from that distant place that the sounds of strings echo in my ears, continually, like a ghostly relic. Let's do a spin. I admire how light you are on your feet. Lionel, who watches the world from his window, loves the gray of the sky as much as I do, at least he's sure, he says, that the weather isn't pleasing anyone at all, and with a little luck, he says, melancholy will manage to overtake an idiot or two and you'll feel a little less alone, a tiny little bit less alone, he says, than on those National Cultural Heritage days when you see clusters of happy people going past in shorts like fat bunches of grapes, shorts should be banned in towns, he says, even in small towns, shorts should be permitted in open country and only in open country, and then only in autumn colors, towns should have a ban on shorts and happy people, he says in conclusion. Every day, Genevieve, we talk on the phone. Every morning we call each other, we almost don't speak to each other anymore except on the phone, we're that close. We no longer need a face to talk to. Tomorrow morning I'll tell Lionel that Arthur has bought himself an apartment in Jerusalem. Maybe he knows and he's had the tact, knowing how coolly I would view it, to keep quiet. I would like to know what Lionel thinks on this matter. And Arthur too, I miss. I miss him. Not just at checkers, where despite the fact that his game had really gone down, he was the only possible partner. Despite the fact that his game had gone down alarmingly, which he did out of friendship, another discipline. I miss him because I laughed with him too. There was a

time when Arthur and I could laugh about the general
failure of life. Arthur, I don't know if you know, almost
separated from Vera because of a dream. He woke up
one morning and said to Vera, "You're horrible. You're
a horrible woman." Vera, in his dream, was taking him
to lunch. Contrary to their usual habits, Vera is driving
the BMW. It's supposed to be midday, but they're driving in twilight down the sandy bed of a dried-up river,
sort of like the Garonne at the end of its course.
They're driving, alone, in some sort of estuary lined
with truck stops, they meet the occasional construc-
tion vehicle, pass a gravel pit that's operating at full
capacity. There are boats pulled up in pools of water
against the banks, you can tell that there's free passage
only once a day, you can tell the tide's going to come
in, suddenly Arthur tries to grab the wheel and yells,
Quicksand—the BMW's going to sink! Vera replies,
All you think about is your damn car, you're such a
gutless wonder, I'm never going to take you anywhere
again. When he wakes up, Arthur analyzes the dream,
he goes back to the sand, the mud, the rising tide, the
gravel, the truck stops pretending to be port taverns,
the smell of fish, he thinks about the twilight, he
thinks about the horrible reaction when he tried to

save the BMW, which is to say their return, which is to say the two of them, and he says to himself, aha, that's where she was taking me to lunch. She was actually taking me to death.

That was my Arthur. Hypersensitive, irrational. Why, at the moment when there's nothing more to lose, should he have to give up all claim to his own capriciousness? Embark on a quest for some sort of sorry coherence, at the moment when he should be shedding all inessentials and constructing a last-minute *self*, however pathetic. What's the point? One day, Genevieve, it was a few years ago, I was driving along the quays at the Cours Albert I, on the opposite sidewalk, a man was skirting the wall, an old man with an astrakhan hat and a beige loden coat. He was walking at the pace old people walk, hands in his pockets, alone with his shadow in the sun. It was my father. I often think about that look, and how he never felt it on him. And I see this image again. An image stripped of its truth. He's in Bagneux too. We won't be lost when we get there, Genevieve. My father was what Dacimiento accuses me of being, a sort of cleanliness freak. His grave at Bagneux is of Euville stone. A white stone, plain, perfect for eternity but gets dirty easily. When I go to visit him, I take a plastic bag with an extra-hard-bristled brush, a sponge, and a bottle of water. And we two talk to each other as well, he says here you are at last, my boy, Colette Waintraub, who has no sense of timing, has left this ridiculous pot of flowers on me, it blew over in the first gust of wind, result, everything's a mess, it's raining, there's soil everywhere, patches under the pebbles, can you still read my name? I tell him you're going to be pleased, Papa, I get out all my stuff, I kneel down, clear everything away, and I start scrubbing, rubbing away with the extra-hard brush, he says that's good, you at least understand me, you're the only one who understands me, I scrub away as hard as I can and he starts giving me orders just the way he used to tell me how to scrub his back or how to clean a bathtub, scrub, little one, there, there, right there, you dirty child, do that bit again, scrub the star, you can see it's clogged up with earth, harder, that's better. I stand up, I wheeze, after all I'm seventy-three years old, I've been bent over in my coat for ten minutes already, I put back the various pebbles on the grave, everything looks wonderful, and then I catch a glimpse of the sides and I see that the sides could do with a cleaning too. I'm saying to myself maybe it's unnecessary—who pays attention to the sides?—when I feel a voice that's getting impatient, oh, no, my friend, you're going to finish it, don't be sloppy, clean the whole thing, and I admit he's right, and I kneel down again and I scrub the whole surround like a madman, the lichen, the mold, the gummed-on leaves, the encrusted earth, and when I finish, exhausted, his grave is like new and I say to him you're happy, and he's happy.

My own son, Genevieve, trots around the globe. He's thirty-eight years old and goes from one point on the map to the other and I don't understand a thing. In the course of these wanderings my son frees himself from his wounds, abandons his storm-tossed soul and his inner lacerations, abandons me, and everything we were is thrown into the pit of oblivion. The road to happiness, Genevieve, is perhaps the road to oblivion. In October he'll be back, we'll see each other, and he will be amiable and patient and gentle. And to begin with I'll be amiable and patient and gentle and I'll say to him where's the sense in all this? And I'll wait for him to take my hand and reply where was the sense of all the rest of it? And then I'd say yes, when you come right down to it, where was the sense in all the rest of it? And we wouldn't say another word and we'd take a walk through the bracken and everything would be in order.

At the beginning, Genevieve, I'll be amiable and patient and gentle, I'll say explain the word *happiness*. You have put down roots in this world, my boy. Tell me, how did you do it? Nancy, dear little saint that she is, however, will already have put me on my guard: Stop provoking him, he doesn't want to be *happy* (and listen to the disdain in that word) he wants *to be in his proper place*. —I'll ask what does that mean, his proper place? —Being in his proper place, Nancy will retort, now that she's so seriously well informed, is more than being happy. It means *freeing yourself up*, it means accepting that the most important thing is balance. It means calibrating your weight and your rhythm, like a planet revolving around the sun. You don't wage battles with the outside world anymore, you no longer feel choked by the things you lack, you can even allow yourself to be sad. Your son, she will say by way of conclusion, is finding his proper place. At the beginning, Genevieve, I'll be amiable and patient and gentle. But how do you remain amiable and patient and gentle when you're being told your only son aspires to be floating in the ether. And how do you behave toward someone whose ideal, whose final goal is *to be in his proper place?* Who in the course of this *quest* (I'm borrowing the vocabulary from the Crusades) has freed himself of his wounds and his torments. What stuff is a man made of, who has freed himself of his wounds? And how does one behave toward someone who claims that from now on he is going to take a more serene view of things? It isn't the serene view of things that wounds you, it's the sheer voluptuous pretentiousness of letting you know. Everything in him is proclaiming his serene view of things, the way he sits on a chair, the way he walks, the way he does everything slowly, the way even his eyes are smooth. His eyes, in which, alas, what I see is not the serene view of things but *indifference*.

I'll say, Where's the sense in all this? But he won't take my hand and he won't say the words I want to hear. There will be no words exchanged almost in silence, no unspoken understanding, no walk through the bracken. What there will be, unfortunately, on the one side is silence, and on the other, evidence of bitterness, evidence of injustice, lack of gentleness, lack of pity. An anatomy of melancholy.

I'll say, Explain the word *happy*.

Desolation

I don't want their paraphrases, I don't want their circumlocutions, I want the unadulterated word in all its terror, I want the word *happy*. I like dancing with you, Genevieve, I like your lightness, your hesitant grace. I would like to make you laugh again. Be patient, I can switch moods as I move from one foot to the other.

He should take me in his arms, he should say come, Papa, I'm taking you with me, your friend Genevieve is right, the end of the road is Bagneux, so come to Mombasa and laugh with your son who's as much of an idiot as the Italians in Chandolin forty years, ago, Papa, I'll scrub your grave the way you scrubbed your father's, I'll take the brush and go several times a year, the stone will sparkle and shine, and you will give me your orders and we'll laugh, and meantime while we wait, come with me, let's play horses, the map will be our board, the place doesn't matter, the only reality is inside us, and stop feeling alone, I'll carry you if you want, I can laugh too, whatever you think, what's the point of it all if you're going to find yourself somewhere between Châlons and the rue Ampère waiting for death to snatch you away, you could just as well have been selling pasta in the South, you love *sugo*, the oil, the olives, the tomatoes and garlic, I don't go chasing happiness but I don't avoid it either, it would be such a great surprise if it popped out from behind a tree and hit us in the eye, like the picturesque, I'll be glad to explain the word *happy* to you, Papa, it's nothing like what you think, happy is laughing the way the two of you used to laugh, the way you laughed at the deathbed of your brother Benjamin when you stroked him and you said how beautiful you are, you're at peace now, and I said you can't actually say he's beautiful, Papa, maybe it would be a good idea to close his mouth before his children get here, and we started to try to close his mouth with a dishcloth, you pushing on his jaw, me tying a knot and then tightening it as hard as I could at the top of his skull, and God how we laughed as we looked at him and you said hey, you didn't blow it, and we were weeping with laughter when his children arrived and his son looked at his father all done up like an Easter egg and looked at us hooting with laughter and said what's going on here? and we had to leave the room, do you remember, Papa, because otherwise we'd totally fall apart, and that's what truth is, that's the only truth, and all the rest is fakery masquerading as seriousness.

He should take me in his arms and say all that

to me, Genevieve, and everything would be in order. So please, my son, keep going with the inventory of laughter.

He should say I remember you, Papa, when you prided yourself on being a king when it came to fast talking, you were getting your first orders of shirts from Korea, your specialty was late delivery, you used to be screaming down the telephone in English, even on Sundays, nobody was allowed into the living room, and next morning you said to your clients the boat will be here in a week and after a fortnight you said the boat has had engine trouble, and then you asked yourself okay what can I think up next and we said say there's been a storm, Papa, and you said yes, good idea, children, there's been a terrible storm, bring me the atlas and let's see where it hit. And when the boat docked you got forty thousand shirts with three-quarter-length sleeves because the sleeve measurements you gave them were taken from the shoulder but the Koreans understood them as being taken from the neck. He should say I remember you, Papa, when you were the king of imprecision, he should say, Genevieve, our childhood home is not deserted, I can still hear a voice yelling, "The first person who complains about anything whatever is going to get his throat cut, I'll do it with my bare hands. Not one of you, you band of parasites, has a stock of forty thousand shirts as unsalable in summer as they are in winter." And later, when we were teenagers, Papa, and you started doing business with Rumania, importing blue jeans, denim jackets, *youth apparel*, as you called it, for mass distribution, and we asked, "Don't you have a sample of straight-leg jeans with buttons, not a zipper?" you said, "Yeah, yeah, I've got those," and we said, "But you're sure they're really tight at the ankle and the fly's the same as you get on Levi's?" and you said, "I've got them," "And are they faded like Wranglers, Papa," and you said, "I've got them, I've got them," "And my size, Papa, are you sure there are samples in my size?" "I've got them in every size," and then you added, "And every color," and we got worried. "What do you mean every color, Papa, real jeans only come in blue," and you cut the discussion off by screaming, "Mine are better!" and right away we knew they were shit, the moment you said mine were better we knew they were shit and we were going to find ourselves with orange bell-bottomed jeans with a zippered fly. What you did at home in the seventies was to cre-

ate a sort of ultimate antichic, *les* BETTER *de* Perlman and Company, just like *les* MUST *de* Cartier.

He should say, Papa, I remember *les* BETTER *de*
Perlman. For years, did I ever wear anything but *les*
BETTER *de* Perlman? Did you take on board what it
would do to me, at an age when you have no idea
whether you're the tiniest bit attractive or quite simply
hideous, to have to go choose your clothes in the ware-
house in Orly, and not ever once be able (the expense
was an outrage) to own a single genuine pair of Levi's,
a single genuine New Man, a single genuine pair of
jeans of any kind, frankly, not to mention anoraks,
shirts, polyester pajamas, and super-Shetlands that felt
like emery boards. You admitted, Papa, that *les* BET-
TER *de* Perlman were absolute shit, you admitted it
years later, before that what you said, if you remember,
was, "Prisunic and Monoprix rip off my collections, I
dress half of France but what's good enough for half of
France isn't good enough for the little Perlmans." You
admitted later that the little Perlmans were dressed like
clowns (*les* BETTER had their fair share of minor
manufacturing errors) and how we laughed the day
you admitted with absolute balls, with absolute balls

and genuine hilarity, that the occasional BETTERs samples that were halfway okay had been too fancy and too expensive for the central buyers for the chains.

What wouldn't I give, Genevieve, for him to tell me you're the king of bad faith, the king of injustice and the king of impatience, I carry them inside me like secret assailants, even though I want to be in my proper place or live like a cork floating on water, you can count on me, I too am a member of the tribe of sons, and when death comes for you it will find me watching over your little empire.

And I would say to him don't let yourself be upset, my boy, by my deplorable rantings, with the people I love, I like to explore the precipice, I like extreme danger. I make myself odious, I make myself utterly ugly to test your affection. When it comes to ugliness, I can scale Everest. He would laugh, Genevieve, just as you're laughing right now, I adore the way you laugh, your laughter is my salvation, he too would laugh and I'd say everything's in order, my boy. Finally it doesn't matter whether you're a cork on the water or a man chasing his own grail. Goulandri, my osteopath, came back from Egypt. You came back and at least you shut up. When Goulandri, after three-quarters of an hour of my mythological massage, gets to the high point of his story and announces that, "So Isis finds Osiris' limbs, all except for the phallus, which has been swallowed by a fish," I beg for mercy. You at least come back and you shut up. For which I'm grateful. Doesn't matter if you were out to save your skin or to live in harmony with who knows what. Doesn't matter if the goal of your wanderings was the genealogy of the gods or your own little sweet self. At least you're not bored. You have nothing to share, nothing to pass on. I approve. If only you didn't have that little superior smirk, that little. . . . I'm feeling dizzy, Genevieve, I'm going to keel over, I have to sit down.

Genevieve, I said, after collapsing on the sofa (while trying to maintain some semblance of a ramrod spine), give me your hand, I'm going under. A guy who was born on the Volga and I'm done in by three shots of Stolichnaya. Your hand is warm, I like holding it. What would Leo say if he could see us? Nighttime in the rue Ampère, listening to Jewish songs and facing down death. The rue Ampère, which you said—and you were right—wasn't a *place*. Where are you, my friend? Are you still out there somewhere, or have you left us for good? One fine day a man is walking cheerfully down a street in Paris, he has the sky, he has the river, he has his old friend—sky, river, old friend—he has the buildings, the doors, the faces, he has (though he doesn't know it) you, Genevieve Abramowitz. You went away, Leo, before defeat could have the last word. The world in its essence, reduced to almost nothing. All his life our friend Lionel has looked at the chestnut tree at the intersection of Laugier and Farraday. Every day, in every season, Lionel looked at this arrogant, detestable tree which doesn't deserve the slightest attention, and which kept up an unceasing litany of I don't give a fuck about you standing up there hunched behind your window, I was alive a long time before you came on the scene and I'll keel over a long time after you do, I dominate you absolutely, my sadness is no sadness, my nakedness is no nakedness, nothing wears me down, nothing fills me with anticipation, and I pity you. As for these Jewish melodies— adieu, you're too gloomy, my son-in-law can play them at my burial. This evening what we want is gaiety,

Desolation

Genevieve. Do you know *The Art of the Fugue*? Counterpoint 13, the thirteenth fugue. My entire life in dance and song. My entire life somehow inexplicably contained in dance and song, and whether I was numb or happy, defeated or upright, somehow inexplicably it always brought me joy. It's so strange to see all this furniture pushed into the corners. As if the line had already been drawn under my balance sheet. For years on this library ladder I played the Indian shot through by an arrow. It wasn't ever enough for me to fall from my full height. They had to have the high rock, the chasm, and the long death rattle. The fleetingness of objects. I haven't stood on that ladder for twenty-five years. Not to play Indians and not to fetch a book. Would you like me to do the Indian shot through by an arrow, Genevieve? There's a danger I'll do it better than ever, given my condition. Don't be afraid, it's really only a matter of two steps up. Best was when I managed to pull off a couple of last convulsions on the floor. The children adored final spasms. I only did them when they had special friends over. Show them, show them how you die! they begged. I'm going to show you how I die, Genevieve

A NOTE ABOUT THE AUTHOR

Yasmina Reza is a playwright and novelist whose plays have all been multi-award-winning critical and popular international successes, translated in more than thirty languages. Her plays include *Conversations After a Burial*, *The Passage of Winter*, *Art* (which was awarded a Tony in 1999), *The Unexpected Man*, and *Life* × 3. She is also the author of a translation of Kafka's *Metamorphosis*; a novel, *Hammerklavier*; and a film, *Lulu Kreutz's Picnic*. She lives in Paris.

A NOTE ABOUT THE TRANSLATOR

Carol Brown Janeway's translations include Binjamin Wilkomirski's *Fragments*, Marie de Hennezel's *Intimate Death*, Bernhard Schlink's *The Reader*, Jan Philipp Reemtsma's *In the Cellar*, Hans-Ulrich Treichel's *Lost*, Zvi Kolitz's *Yosl Rakover Talks to God*, Benjamin Lebert's *Crazy*, and Sándor Márai's *Embers*.

A NOTE ON THE TYPE

The text of this book was set in Electra, a typeface designed by
W. A. Dwiggins (1800–1956). This face cannot be classified as
either modern or old style. It is not based on any historical model,
nor does it echo any particular period or style. It avoids the
extreme contrasts between thick and thin elements that mark
most modern faces, and it attempts to give a feeling
of fluidity, power, and speed.

Composed by Creative Graphics, Allentown, Pennsylvania
Printed and bound by R. R. Donnelley & Sons, Harrisonburg, Virginia
Designed by Iris Weinstein